Dan Gutman

Simon & Schuster Books for Young Readers

New York   London   Toronto   Sydney   Singapore

SIMON & SCHUSTER BOOKS FOR YOUNG READERS
An imprint of Simon & Schuster Children's Publishing Division
1230 Avenue of the Americas, New York, New York 10020

SIMON & SCHUSTER BOOKS FOR YOUNG READERS
is a trademark of Simon & Schuster.

Book design by Ann Sullivan
The text for this book is set in Janson Text.

Printed in the United States of America
2 4 6 8 10 9 7 5 3 1

Photos courtesy of the Library of Congress and Dan Gutman
Map on page 91 by Nina Wallace
Photo on page 102 © 2002 Photosphere Images Ltd.

Library of Congress Cataloging-in-Publication Data
Gutman, Dan.
Qwerty Stevens, stuck in time with Benjamin Franklin / by Dan Gutman.
p. cm.
Summary: After accidentally sucking Benjamin Franklin into the twenty-first-century
New Jersey with his Anytime Anywhere machine, thirteen-year-old Qwerty Stevens
and his best friend almost wind up stuck in Philadelphia on July 4, 1776 when they try
to send him back.
ISBN 0-689-84553-7
[1. Time travel—Fiction. 2. Franklin, Benjamin, 1706-1790—Fiction. 3. Philadelphia
(Pa.)—History—Revolution, 1775-1783—Fiction. 4. Schools—Fiction.] I. Title.
PZ7.G9846 Qw 2002
[Fic]—dc21
2001049725

To the great kids, teachers, and librarians
at schools I visited in 2001

In New Jersey: Stoy in Haddon Hts., Woodmere in Eatontown, Nut Swamp in Middletown, Berlin Community in Berlin, Brookdale in Bloomfield, Shongum in Randolph, Essex Fells in Essex Fells, Reverend Brown in Sparta, Norwood in Norwood, Village in Middletown, James Monroe in Edison, King in Piscataway, Holland Township in Milford, Belhaven in Linwood, Dugan in Marlboro, McGaheran in Lebanon, Jefferson in Maplewood, Fairview in Red Bank, Tomaso in Warren, Clarendon in Secaucus, Merritt Memorial in Cresskill, Solomon Schechter in New Milford, Shull in Perth Amboy, Upper Township in Mamora, Reeds Road in Absecon, and Johnson Park School in Princeton.

In Texas: Barbers Hill in Mont Belvieu, Hardin in Hardin, Newport and Drew Schools in Crosby, Cummings, Klentzman, Alexander, and Youens School in Houston, McRoberts, Hayes, Memorial Parkway, Fielder, Sundown, Golbow, and Cimarron Schools in Katy, Crockett, Fain, Franklin, Cunningham, and Milam Schools in Wichita Falls, Humble and Northbelt Schools in Humble.

In Pennsylvania: Hoover in Langhorne, Second Ave. in Phoenixville, Holland in Holland, St. Joseph in Downingtown, Loomis, Russell, and Worrall Schools in Broomall, Culbertson in Newtown Square, Wallingford in Wallingford, Whitehall-Coplay in Whitehall, Linglestown and Fishing Creek Valley Schools in Harrisburg, St. Catherine of Siena in Reading.

In New York: Pine Tree in Monroe, Heathcote in Scarsdale, Midland, Osborn, and Rye Neck School in Rye, and United Nations International School in New York City.

In Connecticut: Barnard, Whitney, Crandall and Enfield Street Schools in Enfield, Ledyard Center and Gallup Hill Schools in Ledyard, and Barnum School in Groton.

In Tennessee: Washington, Lincoln and Johnson Schools in Kingsport. In North Dakota: Franklin, Phoenix, Lake Agassi, Century and Wilder Schools in Grand Forks. In Florida: Sandy Lane, Davis, Kings Highway, Plumb, and McMullen-Booth Schools in Clearwater. In Alabama: Lincoln Middle in Birmingham, Crestline in Mountain Brook, and Randolph School in Huntsville.

In Ohio: Harmon and Diley Middle Schools in Pickerington. In Maryland: Hampstead and North Carroll School in Hampstead MD, and East Middle School in Westminster. In Oklahoma: Sequoyah, Summit, Central, Cimarron, and Cheyenne Middle Schools in Edmond. In Illinois: Churchill, MacArthur, Nerge, Stevenson, and Muir Schools in Schaumburg.

Acknowledgments

Thanks to Philip McEntee and Ed Mauger,
who were kind enough to read the manuscript and help make
Benjamin Franklin and the events of July 4, 1776, come alive.
Also, thanks to David Kelly of the Library of Congress.

"I have sometimes almost wished it had been my destiny to be born two or three centuries hence . . . "
—Benjamin Franklin

**Everything in this book is true,
except for the stuff I made up.***

*If you want to know which is which,
turn to the "Truths and Lies" section in the back
of the book. But please, read the story first!

To whom it may concern . . .

The machine inside this box is a secret machine. It is the only one of its kind in the world. It is a very powerful machine. If it fell into the wrong hands, there's no telling what might happen. It could change the course of human history. That's why I have written this note and taped it in the box.

I call it the Anytime Anywhere Machine. I found it while I was digging in my backyard, which is next door to Thomas Edison's old laboratory in West Orange, New Jersey. Edison, I learned, invented the Anytime Anywhere Machine in 1879, the same year he invented the incandescent light. He couldn't do anything with the machine back then. But I discovered, when it's interfaced with a personal computer and a modem, the Anytime Anywhere Machine could send a person anywhere in the world and anytime in history—instantly.

Teleportation and time travel are possible, and it took the genius of Thomas Edison to figure it out.

In the event of my death or disappearance, you may have discovered this note. I beg you. Please be very, very careful with the Anytime Anywhere Machine. In the wrong hands, it could be more dangerous than a nuclear weapon.

Do not—I repeat—do not let a man named Ashley Quadrel near the machine. He is trouble.

—Qwerty Stevens

1

Instant Report

"Q-Man!" Joey Dvorak shouted as he bounded up the stairs to Qwerty Stevens's room before school on Tuesday morning. Joey was lugging a large canvas pack on his back that contained a snare drum, which he played in the school orchestra. "You up?"

Qwerty was up, barely. He had thrown on some clothes and fallen back in his bed, half asleep. Middle school started way too early, both boys agreed. Didn't the Board of Education know that teenage boys need more sleep? A ten or eleven o'clock first period would make so much more sense.

"I'm up," Qwerty grunted at Joey. "What's the rush, anyway? If we show up early, we just have to hang around until homeroom."

"Didja finish your report?" Joey asked.

"What report?"

"The report on the American Revolution," Joey informed him. "For social studies. It's due today."

"Next week, dude."

"*Today*, dude," Joey insisted, showing Qwerty the assignment sheet. "And we have the test on Thursday."

Qwerty let out a curse, something he did not do often. He had completely forgotten about the report. The previous night, when he had spent three hours playing computer games, he could have been working on it.

"I can't believe you forgot," Joey said, shaking his head.

"I forgot."

"How could you forget?"

"I don't know. I just did."

"Don't you write stuff down?"

"I forgot to write it down."

Qwerty had never told his best friend—or anybody else at school—that he had a mild learning disability. Lots of other kids had attention deficit disorder, but it wasn't the kind of thing you talked about. You just took your pills, went to your "doctor" appointments ("doctor" meaning "psychologist"), and kept it to yourself. Between clothes, looks, athletic ability, and everything else kids made fun of, there was no point in broadcasting the fact that you were an A.D.D. kid.

Qwerty Stevens was not dumb. In fact, he was one of the "gifted" students at Thomas Edison Middle School in West Orange, New Jersey. Practically a genius with computers and electronics, he could take apart, put together, and fix just about any machine. Some things came very naturally to him. Other things—remembering assignments, organizing his school supplies, tidying up his bedroom—were not his strong points.

Qwerty's room was about as messy as any other seventh grader's. Old toys he hadn't touched in years were scattered around. The corner served as a "hamper" for his dirty clothes. Wires and jacks and assorted computer components were everywhere.

"You gotta turn in *something!*" Joey told his friend. "Miss Vaughn will fail you this time."

"And my mom will kill me," Qwerty added.

Joey was in many ways the direct opposite of Qwerty, but somehow the two boys enjoyed each other's company. Joey just thought of Qwerty as a bit "scatterbrained." Tall and thin, Joey was a straight-A student who showed up fifteen minutes early for wherever he had to be. Joey had a completed, twenty-three-page report in his backpack describing the events that led to America breaking away from England in 1776. He had jazzed up his report with drawings he found in library books. He put the whole thing in a fancy binder. He even used footnotes. It took several weeks to complete the assignment.

Unlike a lot of the kids in the class, Joey thought history and old things were cool. Warfare was fascinating to him. He had seen virtually every war movie ever made. Doing a report on the American Revolution was not *work* for him.

Joey lived with his father, a cold and angry man, so he would leave the house early most mornings to pick up Qwerty. On two occasions Joey ran away from home, but both times he only made it as far as Qwerty's house.

"Robert!" Qwerty's mother hollered up from the kitchen. She insisted on calling him the name she had given him at birth, despite the fact that everyone else called him Qwerty—a nickname based on the top row of letters on the computer keyboard." You've got to leave for school in fifteen minutes!"

"Okay, Mom!" Qwerty called downstairs.

"And don't forget to go straight to your doctor appointment after school."

"Okay, Mom!"

"You're in trouble, aren't you?" Joey asked.

"Not necessarily," Qwerty replied, more calm than desperate. Though he was not a spectacular student, he was a quick thinker, a problem solver. He could usually come up with a solution in a crisis. Maybe not a great solution, but a solution. "I have a plan," he said, throwing Joey a wink.

Qwerty sat down at his computer and flipped it on.

"You can't start writing your report *now*," Joey complained, glancing at the clock radio on Qwerty's night table. "We gotta get to school."

"I'm *not* writing it now," Qwerty assured his friend. He clicked on his modem and typed in his user ID and password to log on to the Internet. The modem beeped and buzzed and bleeped for a few seconds.

"Music to my ears," Qwerty said, chuckling.

Joey shook his head. If *he* had waited until the last minute to do an assignment, he'd be in a panic. He was more nervous about Qwerty's report than Qwerty was.

"The Web is the answer to just about any problem, my man," Qwerty said as the modem made the connection.

Qwerty typed the words AMERICAN REVOLUTION into the search engine, then leaned back in his chair while the computer did its business. A few seconds later, the results of the search appeared on the screen.

"A hundred and eighteen Web sites!" marveled Joey.

"Too general," Qwerty mumbled. He thought for a moment, then typed in 4TH OF JULY.

This time the computer produced fewer sites, but most of them were useless. There were sites that sold fireworks, sites full of Fourth of July greeting cards, even a site with a recipe for Fourth of July cheesecake. Qwerty grunted.

"Try July fourth, seventeen seventy-six," Joey suggested.

It didn't take long for the computer to come up with six sites that fit the description. One of them was a "virtual tour" of Philadelphia on the day

America declared its independence from England.

"Bingo!" Qwerty exclaimed as he clicked on the site.

"WELCOME TO THE CITY OF BROTHERLY LOVE," the home page announced. There were photos of the Liberty Bell, Independence Hall, and the house where Thomas Jefferson wrote the Declaration of Independence.

Qwerty ignored all these, instead clicking on the words STORY OF A REVOLUTION.

What appeared on the screen next were ten pages of plain text that described how the original thirteen colonies were settled, how they grew, why they felt the need to break away from England, and how they won the war for independence. It was all there, and even written by a professional writer.

"Instant report!" Qwerty announced gleefully.

"That's plagiarism, you know," Joey pointed out, slightly annoyed that Qwerty had been able to whip up a report in minutes that was just as good or even better than the one he had worked so hard on.

"Desperate times call for desperate measures."

"What if Miss Vaughn finds out you copied somebody else's report?" Joey asked.

"She's not gonna find out. You worry too much."

"I don't feel good about this," Joey mumbled.

Qwerty selected the ten pages of text and pasted it into a blank word processing document. He deleted the name of the person who had actually written the report and typed his own name in its place. "Hand me that fat book on the third shelf, will you?"

Joey pulled down the book Qwerty had asked for—an encyclopedia of American history that his uncle had given him a few birthdays ago. Qwerty had never opened it before. But now he was leafing through it very purposefully.

"What are you doing?" Joey asked.

"Grabbing a little art," Qwerty explained as he placed the open book facedown on his scanner. "Teachers love that stuff. Maybe Miss Vaughn will give me extra credit."

Joey snorted. Life wasn't fair.

Qwerty hurriedly scanned a picture of one of the Founding Fathers from the book, then cut and pasted it in the middle of the first page of his report. The text automatically wrapped itself around the picture to create a handsome layout. Qwerty turned on his printer and pulled down

PRINT on the menu bar at the top of the screen.

"See? This is why computers are such wonderful tools for education," he joked, punching Joey in the arm. "You never have to do any work again!"

But Joey wasn't laughing. Something very strange and unusual had happened seconds after Qwerty scanned the picture in the book. "Uh . . . Qwerty," Joey said.

"Yeah?" Qwerty was pulling the pages out of the printer as they slid from the slot.

"Uh . . . there's a really old guy sitting on your bed."

"Very funny."

"No, I mean it."

Qwerty turned around to find that his friend really *did* mean it. Incredibly, astonishingly, sitting there at the edge of his bed was a very old man.

2

The Time Suck

"It's almost time for school!" Qwerty's mother hollered from downstairs.

Qwerty shut the door quickly. Normally he could remain quite calm in pressure situations. But this was *different.* An old guy had just appeared out of nowhere and was now sitting on his bed! He and Joey stared for a few seconds, frozen like statues, their mouths hanging open. The old man's eyes were closed.

"Qwerty," Joey finally said, "this dude is asleep!"

So he was. The old man sat there, motionless. He was a large man, somewhat overweight but not quite fat. A long brown coat was wrapped around him, but a ruffled white shirt could be seen underneath it. He had a plain face. On his head was a shapeless coonskin cap, with his long gray hair hanging out in the back. His glasses were two small circles perched on the edge of his nose. In his right hand was a white cane.

"M-maybe he's dead!" Qwerty stammered. "I have a dead body in my room!"

"What did you do?"

"I don't know!"

"Well, how did he get here?"

"How should I know?"

"Wait, I think he's breathing," Joey said, relieved.

"He might be homeless," Qwerty worried out loud.

"Nah, his clothes are too nice."

"Look," Qwerty pointed out, "he's wearing tights! That's sick!"

"Who cares what he's wearing? We're in trouble! What are we gonna do with this guy? We have to go to school."

"Maybe we can stick him in my closet."

"You can't stick him in your closet!"

"You're right," Qwerty agreed. "My closet is filled with junk."

At that moment, the old man on the bed opened his eyes. They were brown, and friendly. He looked at the boys. They stared back at him.

"What's your name, dude?"

The old man looked at the boys a moment longer before delivering a response. "Franklin is the name," he said, "Benjamin Franklin."

Several weeks earlier, Qwerty had dug up the Anytime Anywhere Machine in his backyard.

After his adventure with the great inventor Thomas Edison (he almost didn't make it home), Qwerty doubted he would ever use the machine again.

For those few moments, the two boys had forgotten about the Anytime Anywhere Machine, which was hooked up to Qwerty's computer by cables and hidden under his bed. For those moments, they weren't thinking about the picture Qwerty had scanned into the computer, or the Fourth of July Web site. All they could think of was that there was an old man—who smelled vaguely of talcum powder and claimed to be Benjamin Franklin—sitting on Qwerty's bed. He had appeared, seemingly, out of thin air.

"If you're Benjamin Franklin," Qwerty snorted, "I'm Elvis Presley."

"It is then my pleasure to make your acquaintance, Master Presley."

"Wait a minute," Joey interrupted. "You mean to say you're the Benjamin Franklin who invented bifocals and the Franklin stove? The guy who discovered lightning?"

"The lightning was always there, young man," Franklin said, his eyes twinkling. "I merely claim to have proved that lightning and electricity are one and the same."

"He does look like Benjamin Franklin," Joey commented. "He's on the hundred-dollar bill, you know."

"Oh, yeah?" Qwerty said. "This guy could be anybody. *Prove* you're Benjamin Franklin."

"A man that knows himself I never knew," Franklin said. "Master Presley, there are three things extremely hard: steel, a diamond, and to know one's self."

"I think he *is* Benjamin Franklin!" Joey exclaimed. "The Anytime Anywhere Machine must have sucked him through time and brought him here!"

"A time suck!" Qwerty marveled. "Who would have thought it was possible?"

Benjamin Franklin sat there, a quizzical smile on his face, as Qwerty got down on his hands and knees to reach under his bed. "I must have hit the on/off switch with my foot when I woke up!"

Joey picked up the lid of the scanner and took out the book. The portrait that Qwerty had scanned was of Benjamin Franklin.

"An excellent likeness, don't you think?" Franklin asked as he looked over Joey's shoulder at the page. He had an easy laugh.

Qwerty sat on his chair with a thud. "I can't believe I brought Benjamin Franklin here."

"We gotta send him back, dude! You can't be sucking people out of their own time and zapping them around in history. This is dangerous."

"I know. I know."

"One moment," Franklin said, struggling to his

feet. Standing, he was taller than either of the boys, about five feet ten inches. "Where am I?"

"West Orange, New Jersey," Qwerty replied.

"Not Philadelphia?"

"We're about a hundred miles north of Philadelphia."

"But a trip of such distance takes several days by even the swiftest rider. I don't recall even summoning my horse."

"I have this machine," Qwerty explained. "The Anytime Anywhere Machine. It can transport a person to any location, any time in history . . . instantly."

Franklin thought about that for a moment, not quite comprehending.

"What century is it?" Franklin asked, looking around the room.

"The twenty-first," Joey replied.

Franklin sat down on the bed again, stunned.

"Are New Jersey and Pennsylvania still colonies?" he asked, almost in a whisper.

"No," Joey replied.

Franklin's shoulders sagged visibly.

"They're states."

"States?" Franklin asked, leaning forward with excitement.

"They're part of the United States of America," Qwerty added.

"The United States," Franklin said, letting the words roll off his tongue as if he was hearing them for the first time. "I like the sound of that. So the revolution will be successful?"

Qwerty and Joey looked at each other. "You don't know?" they asked simultaneously.

Franklin shook his head. "I had wondered how it would turn out," he said.

"What date do you think it is?" Joey asked.

"July the fourth, in the year seventeen seventy-six," Franklin replied. "What am I doing here?"

"Let's just say it was a little accident," Qwerty explained. "Not a big deal. We'll just send you right back to where you came from. No problem at all."

Qwerty sat down at the computer and began fiddling with the mouse as Franklin looked over his shoulder curiously. "What is this machine, Elvis?" he asked.

"A computer."

"It computes numbers?"

"Not just numbers," Qwerty explained. "It can manipulate pictures, words, sounds, just about anything."

"Ingenious!"

At that moment, Qwerty's bedroom door opened. It was his six-year-old sister Madison. Or, as Qwerty called her, "Thing 2." Madison was all dressed up for school, wearing the Barbie backpack she had picked out at the start of first grade. She didn't seem to notice Franklin right away.

"Can I play with the computer after school?" Madison asked Qwerty.

"No, Thing Two. You'll wreck it."

"Hmphf," Madison snorted, crossing her arms in front of her. "Then I'm not going to be your friend anymore, and you can't come to my birthday party!"

"Good morning, little girl," Franklin said cheerfully.

"Who's the old man?" Madison asked.

"He's . . . my imaginary friend," Qwerty replied, desperately wishing he had come up with something better. "He can be your imaginary friend, too. Just as long as you don't tell Mom and Dad about him."

"He doesn't look imaginary to me," Madison insisted. "He looks real."

"Delightful child!" Franklin exclaimed.

"Imaginary friends always look real," Joey told

Madison. "That's why they're so convincing."

"I don't believe you," Madison said, narrowing her eyes.

"There are but three faithful friends," Franklin said. "An old wife, an old dog, and ready money."

"Look, I'll give you ice cream if you keep your mouth shut," Qwerty told his sister.

"Okay . . . but how will I eat it with my mouth shut?" She giggled, skipping out of the room. Qwerty let out a sigh of relief.

While Qwerty was negotiating with his sister, Benjamin Franklin got up and went over to examine the desk lamp on Qwerty's night table. He put his face right next to the bulb and looked at it with a puzzled expression on his face. "It appears to produce both light and heat, but no flame," the old inventor marveled. "How is this possible?"

Joey flipped the switch to turn the light off, then flipped it again to turn it back on.

Franklin jumped back with a start. "Ingenious!" he exclaimed, never taking his eye off the bulb. "My father, Josiah, was a candle maker. He once attempted to make a smokeless candle, but alas was unsuccessful. It appears that this has now been accomplished."

Hesitantly, Franklin reached out and slowly

flipped the switch to turn the light off. Then he turned it on again. Then off again. He looked like a baby who had just been given a new toy. "Where is the flame?" he asked.

"There is no flame," Qwerty explained. "It's electric. You see, there's this filament in the bulb, and when you flip the switch, it shoots electricity through the filament to make it glow."

"Filament, eh?" Franklin said. Having spent years studying electricity, his experiments had made him one of the most famous men in the world. "I am much in the dark about light. How does one obtain the electric fire? I see no electrical batteries in this room. Must you wait for a storm?"

Qwerty and Joey looked at each other. Neither boy had any idea how electricity was produced.

"They've got these, uh, generators," Qwerty tried to explain, "and they spin around—"

"At Niagara Falls or someplace," Joey added. "And they send the electricity over power lines to each house."

"And my mom and dad are constantly telling me to turn the lights off when I leave a room, because they get a bill at the end of each month for the electricity they used."

"Yeah," Joey agreed.

"Fascinating!" enthused Franklin, still flipping the light on and off. "Who invented this marvelous electric light?"

"Thomas Edison," the boys answered together.

"He must be an extraordinary man," Franklin said.

"Oh he *is*," Qwerty agreed. "I mean, he *was*."

"Listen, Mr. Franklin, we'd better get you back home," Joey said. "You have a lot of important things to do, it being July fourth in seventeen seventy-six and all."

"They can wait," Franklin replied, turning his attention to the next mysterious device on Qwerty's night table. "What is this machine?"

"It's a clock radio," Qwerty explained. "See, you set the time on the clock, and when that time arrives, the radio clicks on."

Qwerty pushed a button, and music came out of the radio. Franklin, who had never seen a digital clock or heard a radio, jumped back with fear and covered his face. Qwerty quickly turned it off.

"What was *that?*" the astonished Franklin asked.

"Heavy metal," Qwerty replied.

"Are there . . . people in there?" Franklin asked, peering at the radio closely.

"No," Qwerty chuckled. "It's electric. It captures radio waves that are in the air and turns them into sound."

"Ingenious!" Franklin exclaimed. "And what is this?"

"It's a pencil sharpener," Qwerty said as he stuck a pencil into the hole, ground the end to a point, and held it up for Franklin to see.

"Astonishing!" Franklin said as he looked inside the pencil sharpener. "Also electric?"

"Yes," Joey said impatiently. "Mr. Franklin, we really must get you back to Philadelphia. The revolution and all . . ."

"Haste makes waste," Franklin said. "What is this machine, Elvis?"

"That's my air conditioner," Qwerty told him.

"It conditions the air? Fascinating! And all these machines use electric fire? I had no idea that one day this spark would be put to such varied purposes."

Franklin moved excitedly about Qwerty's room, flipping every switch and pressing every button he could find.

"To what purpose does this serve?" he kept asking. Qwerty had never realized how many electrical appliances he had in his room.

Joey, meanwhile, was getting nervous. It was

time to go to school. He didn't like being late for things. More importantly, they had to return Benjamin Franklin to July 4, 1776, to sign the Declaration of Independence. The guy was, after all, one of the "Founding Fathers" of America.

It was while Franklin was attempting to "turn on" the stapler that Qwerty had a brainstorm. It was such a simple, brilliant idea that Qwerty couldn't help but grin at his own sheer genius. "Hey," he said, "let's bring Mr. Franklin to school with us!"

"No! No way, José! Out of the question! Bad move! Don't even *think* about it!" was Joey's response.

"Why not?" Qwerty argued. "He's not in any big rush to get back to Philadelphia. I could take him into Miss Vaughn's class with me. It will be like part of my report. She *told* us to be creative. She *said* we could use audiovisual aids. Teachers love that stuff. She'll probably give me extra credit for originality."

"You're out of your mind!" Joey complained.

"Oh, come on. You just wish *you'd* thought of it."

"Do not!"

"Do too!"

Nobody had asked Benjamin Franklin what *he* thought of the idea. They didn't need to.

"Marvelous idea!" he said, "Accompanying you to your school would be a most educational experience for *me*. I founded an institution of higher learning, myself. I would be more than curious to see how American education has advanced in the last two centuries."

"Cool!" Qwerty said.

"We're gonna get in so much trouble," said Joey, slapping his forehead.

It was then that the bedroom door opened once again. This time it was Qwerty's older sister, Barbara. Or, as Qwerty called her, "Thing 1." Barbara was a sophomore in high school.

"Madison told me—" Barbara stopped in her tracks at the sight of Benjamin Franklin. "Oh my God!"

"It was an accident!" Qwerty assured his sister, shutting the door so his mother would not hear what was going on. Except for Joey, Barbara was the only other person who knew about the Anytime Anywhere Machine.

"Qwerty, are you crazy?" Barbara asked.

"Your brother did a time suck," Joey said.

"A what?"

"The Anytime Anywhere Machine sucked him out of his time and into our time."

"It's Benjamin Franklin," explained Qwerty weakly.

"I *know* it's Benjamin Franklin!" Barbara exploded. "Of *course* it's Benjamin Franklin! Who else *could* it be but Benjamin Franklin! I can't believe you would do something so stupid as to use the Anytime Anywhere Machine to bring Benjamin Franklin here! Mom and Dad are going to kill you!"

"I didn't mean to!"

"So my reputation precedes me!" Franklin said gallantly as he took Barbara's hand and brought it to his lips. "To what do I owe the presence and pleasure of this sweet young flower?"

Barbara looked at the old man, first with surprise, next with suspicion, and finally with a hint of a smile. None of the boys *she* went out with ever kissed her hand. If any of them ever so much as opened a door for her, she probably would have dropped dead from the shock. "I'm Barbara," she said with a curtsy. "His sister."

"Barbara," Franklin repeated, bowing deeply. "A lovely name. I shall remember it for eternity, and particularly when what hair I have remaining on my head is shorn."

Joey was the only one who got Franklin's little

pun. "Barber . . . Barbara," he said to the others.

Barbara laughed. "Oh, Mr. Franklin!"

Qwerty shook his head in disbelief. *My sister is flirting with Benjamin Franklin*, he thought to himself. *The guy is like four times her age!* "Knock it off, Barb!" he hissed.

"He's cute," she replied, giggling.

Joey had been looking at Qwerty's clock with growing impatience. They couldn't wait any longer, he decided. If he was going to avoid being marked tardy, he would have to take control of the situation. At this point, there was no longer time to get Franklin back to 1776. They would have to take him to school with them. "Barbara, this is an emergency," Joey said. "We need your help."

"What do you want me to do?"

"Go downstairs and distract your mom and dad so we can get Mr. Franklin out of the house without them seeing him," Joey said. "Will you do that?"

"Where are you taking him?" Barbara asked.

"Don't worry about that," Qwerty said. "We'll take care of him."

"Well, okay," Barbara agreed reluctantly. "But you guys owe me, big time. And he'd better be gone by the time Mom and Dad get home from work tonight."

"I pray we might have the pleasure of a second encounter before I take my leave of here, fair Barbara," Franklin said, bowing again.

"Bye-bye, Ben!" she giggled with another curtsy, before dashing out of the room.

Barbara went down to the kitchen, where her mother and father were eating breakfast and getting ready to go to work. Madison had already been picked up for school by one of the carpool moms.

"What's taking Qwerty and Joey so long?" Mrs. Stevens asked Barbara.

"They're coming," Barbara replied. "I think they're cleaning up Qwerty's room or something."

"That would be a first," Mr. Stevens snorted from behind his newspaper.

"Boys!" Mrs. Stevens shouted. "Don't you want a little breakfast?"

"No time, Mom!" Qwerty yelled back. He and Joey had each grabbed one of Franklin's arms and were hustling the old man down the stairs. When they were halfway down, Mrs. Stevens suddenly appeared in the front hallway. Qwerty and Joey pushed their way in front of Franklin, obscuring any view of the old man from below. Franklin, for a change, held his tongue.

"Don't forget your doctor appointment after school," Mrs. Stevens reminded Qwerty. "You'd better write it down."

"I will, Mom."

Barbara knew there was no way for her brother to get Franklin out of the house with their mother standing at the bottom of the stairs.

"Ohhhhhh!" she moaned from the kitchen, "I'm going to be sick! I think I have to throw up!"

Mr. and Mrs. Stevens ran to Barbara, who was bent over the sink, doing her best impersonation of someone struck by a sudden, violent stomach virus.

"Get her a glass of water!" Mrs. Stevens ordered her husband.

"You'll be okay, sweetie," assured Mr. Stevens.

While his parents were busy giving Barbara medical attention, Qwerty and Joey hustled Franklin down the stairs and out the front door.

3

Extra Credit

Thomas Edison Middle School was just a few
blocks from the Stevens' residence. It was a short
walk for most people. But Benjamin Franklin, well
into his seventieth year and suffering from a
severe case of the gout, moved slowly and cautiously.

"That was close," Joey said, taking Franklin's
elbow to steady him. "I was sure your mom would
see us."

"I do hope your sister will recover from her
sudden ailment," Franklin told Qwerty. "We
abandoned her in a time of need, I fear."

"She was faking it," Qwerty explained. "She

was just distracting my parents so we could get you out of the house."

"Marvelous young lady!"

A black sport-utility vehicle roared around the corner. Franklin, first catching a glimpse of it from the corner of his eye, collapsed with terror. He would have fallen to the ground if Qwerty and Joey had not been holding his arms.

"Sweet mercy!" Franklin shouted. "What in the name of the Lord was that monstrosity?"

"It was a car," Qwerty told him calmly. "It won't hurt you. We drive them around to get from place to place."

"These cars, as you call them," Franklin asked when he had recovered his composure, "do they use electricity, like the previous machines?"

"They burn gasoline," Joey said. When Franklin appeared not to understand, Joey added, "oil," which seemed to ring a bell with the old man.

"Where are the horses?" Franklin asked.

"Most people drive cars these days," Qwerty informed him.

A plane passed overhead and Franklin, still recovering from the shock of seeing his first automobile, reeled backward once again in fright.

"Heaven help us!" the terrified Franklin hollered. "A beast is falling from the sky! Seek shelter!"

"Calm down," Joey said, holding Franklin up once again. "It's only an airplane. When we need to travel long distances, it's faster to fly than it is to drive."

"People . . . fly?" Franklin asked in disbelief. "Elvis, you must explain the physics of these occurrences."

"These two brothers named Wilbur and Orville Wright invented the airplane," Qwerty said. "It was like a hundred years ago or something."

"The world is changed in so many ways," Franklin said wistfully.

"Well, you've been dead for a long time," Qwerty remarked.

By this time, Thomas Edison Middle School was in sight. The late bell had rung, and the students had already filed inside the building. That was somewhat of a relief to Qwerty, who had been wondering how he was going to explain Benjamin Franklin to the tough guys who usually hang out in front of the school. He had once shown up with a different *haircut* and they'd never let him forget it. Qwerty and Joey helped Franklin up the front steps.

"Don't flip out if you set off the metal detector," Qwerty advised Franklin. "It won't hurt you."

"Metal detector?" Franklin asked. "It detects heavy metal, I presume?"

"No," Joey said. "Guns, knives, stuff like that."

Franklin shrugged. All three made it past the metal detector, although Franklin had to remove his shoes when it was discovered they had metal buckles on them. The school secretary stared when Qwerty signed Franklin into the visitors book at the office.

"Are you here for an assembly?" she asked.

"Yes, he is," Qwerty said before Franklin could answer. The boys hustled Franklin out of the office and down the hall to Room 113.

Miss Vera Vaughn had been teaching social studies so long, she remembered the days when kids were taught that Native Americans were called "Indians" and Christopher Columbus "discovered" America. She was pushing seventy-five, suffering from arthritis, and had been eligible for retirement years ago, but she always said they would have to drag her out of the school kicking and screaming. Even though kids called her Turkey Neck and other rude names behind her back, she still loved teaching.

But one thing Miss Vaughn did *not* love was tardiness.

"You're two minutes late," she said sharply when Qwerty and Joey walked into Room 113. A short, pudgy boy was standing at the front of the room holding a binder full of papers as if he was reading to the class. On the blackboard behind him were the words AMERICAN REVOLUTION: REPORTS DUE <u>TODAY.</u> TEST ON THURSDAY.

Franklin stepped in the doorway. All eyes turned to him. "We were detained," he announced. "Please accept my most sincere apology."

"Whoa!" one of the boys in the back of the room exclaimed. "Who's the old dude?"

"He looks like a hippie," one of the other boys decided. "He's a refugee from the sixties. Peace and love. Groovy! Right on!"

"You are such a moron, Marshall," a girl with long brown hair said. "He's not a hippie. He's from, like, France or something."

"Nice hat, dude!" somebody shouted, causing the rest of the class to crack up.

"What matters is what one has inside his head," Franklin said. "Not on top of it."

Franklin didn't appear to be offended by the remarks. In fact, he seemed amused by them. The pudgy boy at the front of the class looked relieved that he was no longer the center of attention.

"Quiet!" Miss Vaughn hollered. "Qwerty, what's going on?"

"Who is this Qwerty?" Franklin asked. "You said your name was Elvis Presley."

The class exploded in laughter again.

"Miss Vaughn, you told us we could use audio-visual aids in our report," Qwerty said, putting his written report on top of the pile the rest of the class had created. "I'm sorry we were late. I'd like to introduce a friend of mine, Mr. Benjamin Franklin."

"That's not fair!" complained Antonia Evers, generally acknowledged to be the smartest and most competitive student in the class. On her desk was a re-creation of the Battle of Bunker Hill that she had constructed in a shoe box. "I didn't know we could hire actors."

"He's not an actor," insisted Joey.

"And I didn't hire him," Qwerty said.

"I see no problem with bringing someone in to portray a historical figure," Miss Vaughn said, softening somewhat. "Mr. Franklin, you may take a seat in the back until it is Qwerty's turn."

Qwerty and Joey took their usual seats next to one another. Franklin didn't sit down at first. Instead, he made his way to Miss Vaughn's desk and bowed graciously before her. "Madam," he said, "it is my pleasure and honor to meet a member of the educational community. For without education, genius is like silver in the mine. And it is especially a pleasure to meet a woman who possesses such beauty as yourself."

Franklin took Miss Vaughn's hand and kissed it.

"*Oooooooooooooooooooooooh,*" went the class.

"Gross!" groaned one of the boys in the back of the room.

"Single and separate, man and woman are like two odd halves of scissors. But together . . ."

"*Oooooooooooooooooooooooh!*"

"Mr. Franklin!" gushed Miss Vaughn, all blushing and embarrassed.

Franklin didn't let go of her hand. "Your husband is a very lucky man," he said, staring into her eyes.

"I have never been married," Miss Vaughn replied.

"Then perhaps it is I who is a lucky man," Franklin proclaimed.

"*Oooooooooooooooooooooooooh!*"

"Oh man," Joey whispered to Qwerty, "I can't believe he's hitting on Miss Vaughn!"

"You are very charming," Miss Vaughn said, removing her hand from Franklin's grasp. "Would you take a seat in the back, Mr. Franklin? Herbie was in the middle of his report when you came in. Herbie, please continue."

Franklin bowed again and took a seat. Herbie Dunn—the pudgy kid—read from the papers he was holding.

"The American colonists got along real good with England for a long time, but then the British government started acting like real jerks, making them pay taxes and stuff and treating them all mean and everything. So the Americans said they wouldn't take it anymore—"

"Excuse me," Franklin said, rising from his seat.

"Yes?" Miss Vaughn asked.

"If I may be so bold," Franklin said, walking to the front of the class. "My fellow colonists do not object to the paying of taxes. On the contrary, as I have many times said, in this world nothing is certain but death and taxes. Our objections were due to the fact that the colonies were not permitted to have representatives in the British Parliament. Those who have no voice nor vote in the electing of representatives do not enjoy liberty but are absolutely enslaved to those who have votes."

"That is correct," Miss Vaughn said, smiling at Franklin. Revolutionary War history was a special interest of hers, and she appreciated when somebody knew his facts. Franklin bowed and went back to his seat.

Herbie continued reading his report. "The first battle took place at Lexington and Concord, in Massachusetts, on April nineteenth, seventeen seventy-five. The British soldiers wanted to take away all the gunpowder from the colonists, but Paul Revere rode his horse through the night to warn everybody that the British were coming. By the time the British soldiers showed up, the American minutemen were there and they killed them all . . ."

Franklin rose from his seat once again. This time he did not request permission to speak.

"Your story is well told and entertaining, young man. However, I feel duty bound to correct several inaccuracies in this account of these events. Mr. Revere, the Boston silversmith, is an excellent rider and a fine patriot. But he never made it to his destination on the evening of April eighteenth."

"He didn't?" Joey asked, genuinely surprised.

"A British patrol intercepted him and took possession of his horse," Franklin revealed. "Mr. Revere walked home that evening."

"Then how did the minutemen know the British were coming?" Herbie asked.

"Mr. Revere was only one of several riders that evening. One of them—thankfully—got to Lexington. A few dozen ragtag rebels were on hand to face seventy British soldiers. The commander of the redcoats ordered the rebels to lay down their guns and go home. They refused to surrender their weapons. A second order was issued, and again they refused. A shot was fired—we know not by whom. When the shooting concluded, a mere five minutes later, eight Americans lay dead, and ten were wounded. One redcoat was hit—on the leg."

"So we actually *lost* the battle?" Joey asked, puzzled.

"No," Franklin said. "The redcoats marched triumphantly up the road to Concord. By that time, their element of surprise had vanished. A large group of militia lay in wait. The redcoats commenced to search houses for hidden ammunition. Little was found, as it had been moved. In their frustration, redcoats burned down the courthouse, which enraged the rebels. They opened fire. Huddled behind rocks and trees, they took down the redcoats one by one. The British retreated, and the rebels gave chase, firing all the way. By the time they reached Boston, the tally counted 270 dead or wounded Englishmen. Our casualties numbered less than one hundred. That is what, in truth, happened."

A hush fell over the class.

"Would you excuse me for a moment?" Miss Vaughn asked Franklin. "There's somebody I want you to meet."

Miss Vaughn left the room, and all the students looked at Franklin expectantly. They wanted to see what he would be like when he wasn't "doing Benjamin Franklin." Franklin looked around the room, taking a special interest in anything that looked like it might be an electrical appliance.

"Hey, old man," a boy in the back called, "how do you know so much about this Revolutionary War stuff?"

"Experience is a dear teacher," Franklin

replied. "Only fools will learn from no other."

"Where'd you get that costume," asked Matt Mehorter, a first-class troublemaker who had already been suspended from school more than once, "from a garbage can? I wouldn't be caught dead in that outfit."

"Having been poor is no shame," said Franklin, "but being ashamed of it, is. And tart words make no friends, young man. A spoonful of honey will catch more flies than a gallon of vinegar."

"Why don't you get a real job?" snorted Matt.

"The worst wheel on the cart makes the most noise," Franklin chuckled. "Half-wits talk much but say little."

"*Ooooooooooooooooooooooooh!*"

"Dude, you can drop the act now," Matt said. "Turkey Neck is out of the room."

"Leave him alone," challenged Qwerty. "He's not bothering you."

"Yeah," Joey agreed, but not very loudly. He had already been in one fight with Matt Mehorter, and he had come away from it with a bloody nose.

"I say this guy's a phony," Matt said, getting up from his seat. He was a big boy, bigger than many men. "I say he made up all that stuff about that battle. I know so."

"Those who profess to know everything," Franklin said calmly, "and so undertake to explain everything often remain ignorant of many things that others could and would instruct them in, if they appeared less conceited. In my view, people who are wrapped up in themselves make small packages."

"*Oooooooooooooooooooooooooh!*"

"Hey, the old man is cool!" somebody said.

Each time the class reacted to one of Franklin's remarks, Matt Mehorter got more red in the face.

"Maybe you'd talk normal if I put my fist in your face," Matt said, taking a step toward Franklin.

"Anger is never without a reason," Franklin replied. "but seldom with a good one."

"Mr. Franklin, just ignore him!" Joey warned.

But Benjamin Franklin was not the type of man to back away when challenged. "Any fool can criticize, condemn, and complain," he said. "And most fools do."

"*Oooooooooooooooooooooooooh!*"

"Are you calling me a fool, you old fool?" Matt was only a few steps away from the old man. Qwerty and Joey rushed to get between Franklin and Mehorter.

"It is hard for an empty bag to stand upright," Franklin remarked, staring at Matt.

"What did he mean by *that?*" Matt asked one of his buddies.

"I don't know, but I think he just put down your mother, dude!"

Matt looked like he was about to haul off and sock Franklin when the door opened and Miss Vaughn returned to class. She was with Dr. Doris Pullman, the principal of Thomas Edison Middle School. Not even forty years old, Dr. Pullman was one of the youngest middle-school principals in the state. Matt, Qwerty, and Joey returned to their seats, pretending that nothing had happened.

"Dr. Pullman," said Miss Vaughn, "I would like to introduce you to Mr.—"

"Franklin is the name," Franklin said, taking the principal's hand and kissing it lightly. "But a woman as ravishingly lovely as yourself must surely address me as Benjamin."

"Aren't I a little young for you, Mr. Franklin?" Dr. Pullman asked with a smile.

"All cats look gray in the dark," Franklin replied.

"*Ooooooooooooooooooooooooh!*"

"Oh man!" Qwerty whispered to Joey, "Now he's hitting on the principal!"

"Perhaps at dismissal you might join me for tea and conversation?" Franklin asked Dr. Pullman, kissing her hand again.

"I don't think my husband would appreciate that very much!"

"You needn't bring him along!" chuckled Franklin.

"*Oooooooooooooooooooooooh!*"

"We gotta get him out of here," Joey whispered to Qwerty.

Dr. Pullman, however, didn't seem to be bothered in the least by Franklin's affection. In fact, she seemed to enjoy it, blushing and smiling like a schoolgirl who had just been asked to dance. Women of all ages, it seemed, found the old man irresistable.

"Miss Vaughn tells me you really know your stuff," Dr. Pullman gushed. "We would be most interested in hiring you to do an assembly as Benjamin Franklin for the whole school. How much do you charge for a full day?"

"Money never made a man happy," Franklin replied, still clutching Dr. Pullman's hand. "The more a man has, the more he wants. Wealth is not his that has it, but his that enjoys it. He that is of the opinion money will do everything may well be suspected of doing everything for money. He does not possess wealth, it possesses him—"

"Oh, I get it!" Dr. Pullman laughed. "You're not allowed to go out of character while you're on the job. What's the best way to reach you? Can you give me your e-mail address?"

"E-mail? I am not familiar with this term. But as postmaster general of the colonies, I pride myself on the rapidity of the mails," Franklin boasted. "Your correspondence will arrive in my eager hand three or four weeks after you post it, my dear. Perhaps a bit longer in the winter months. Poor roads, I'm sure you understand."

"You are just a *darling* man!" bubbled Dr. Pullman as she pinched Franklin's cheek. She told Miss Vaughn that she had to go to a meeting, pulled her hand away from Franklin, and left.

Qwerty and Joey, feeling that Franklin may have overstayed his welcome, rushed to the front of the room and grabbed Franklin by his arms. "Miss Vaughn," Qwerty said, "we have to take Mr. Franklin back to his—"

"Talent agency," Joey contributed.

"Yeah, they only let me have him for an hour.

He's got another, uh, gig he has to do."

"Oh, didn't you drive your car here?" Miss Vaughn asked.

"Goodness no!" exclaimed Franklin. "Any sane man would refuse to climb into one of those contraptions!"

"Ahaha!" giggled Miss Vaughn. "You are fabulous! Qwerty, because you showed such originality, I'm going to give you extra credit for your report. And I'm so pleased that you didn't wait until the last minute to do it this time."

"Never leave that till tomorrow which you can do today," said Franklin cheerfully.

"We gotta go," Joey said with a grimace.

"I'll write you boys a pass," Miss Vaughn said. "Make sure you get 'Mr. Franklin' to wherever he needs to go. And don't forget about the test on this material on Thursday."

She handed Qwerty a slip of paper and shook hands with Franklin. "It has been a pleasure meeting you, sir."

"The pleasure, my dear, was entirely mine," Franklin replied, planting another kiss on her hand. "Happiness consists more in small conveniences that occur every day, than in great pieces of good fortune that happen seldom to a man in the course of his life. Until we have the pleasure again, I shall keep your face in my memory as a reminder of your beauty. I bid you adieu."

"*Ooooooooooooooooooooooooh!*"

On that, Qwerty, Joey, and Benjamin Franklin left the room.

4

The Anytime Anywhere Machine

All in all, Qwerty felt that bringing Benjamin Franklin to school with him had been a good idea. True, Matt Mehorter almost beat the old guy up. True, Franklin seemed to have a little too much fondness for the ladies. But he was a pretty cool guy. And Qwerty got extra credit for his assignment, which certainly didn't happen every day. He was wearing a smile as he and Joey helped Franklin down the front steps of the school.

Joey, on the other hand, was focusing on what *could* have happened. Franklin could have fallen down and broken his hip or something. Matt Mehorter could have killed him with one punch.

Miss Vaughn could have slapped him in the face for coming on to her. Dr. Pullman could have had him arrested.

"Mr. Franklin," Joey said as they headed back to Qwerty's house, "I know you're a lot older than me and all, but I have to tell you that you can't be saying all those things to women in the twenty-first century."

"What things?"

"You know, telling them how beautiful they are, kissing their hand, and stuff. Women don't go for that anymore. I was afraid the principal was going to call security or something."

"Let the fair sex be assured that I shall always treat them with the utmost decency and respect," Franklin said. "If this be an age which shuns the good manners of well-intentioned and deserved compliments, I regret the loss of your civilization."

"Well, nowadays they call those kinds of compliments 'harassment,'" Joey said.

"Lighten up," Qwerty told his friend. "He didn't hurt anybody, and nobody hurt him. Besides, we've got a pass that will get us out of school for as long as we want. Life is good."

Along the way to Qwerty's house, Franklin

stopped here and there to observe things he'd never seen before: a man riding a bicycle; telephone lines overhead; somebody pushing a lawnmower. For a long time he stood and stared watching a traffic light turn from green to yellow to red and back to green again. Everything, in Franklin's opinion, was "ingenious," "remarkable," and "astonishing."

Qwerty's mother and father were both at work, so the boys could enter the house without having to hide Franklin. The old man told them he was hungry and tired, so Qwerty told him to go upstairs and relax while he and Joey prepared something for him to eat.

"We gotta get him out of here," Joey whispered in the kitchen as soon as Franklin was out of earshot.

"What's the rush?" asked Qwerty, poking around in the refrigerator. "He's having a good time. My folks won't be back until dinnertime. Let him stick around for a while. He's a lot of laughs."

"Laughs?!" Joey said. "You never know what crazy thing he might do next! He might accidentally break some law and get thrown in jail! He might be up in your room right now sticking his finger in a light socket to see what happens.

Besides, he was in July fourth, seventeen seventy-six before you time-sucked him here. We could be totally messing up American history by keeping him here."

"You worry too much," Qwerty told his friend. He stuffed some Pop-Tarts in his pocket and poured a bowl of cornflakes for Franklin. "He's not going to get into any more trouble."

"I hope you're right," Joey said as they carried the food upstairs.

When they opened Qwerty's door, Franklin was sitting at the edge of Qwerty's bed, asleep, just as he had been when he first arrived. But this time, Benjamin Franklin was totally naked.

"Whoa!"

Ordinarily, the sight of a totally naked, elderly man sitting on one's bed might make most teenage boys collapse into a fit of uncontrollable giggles. But with the man being Benjamin Franklin in the twenty-first century and the boys being Qwerty Stevens and Joey Dvorak, hilarity was the furthest thing from their minds. *Panic* would be a better word for what they were feeling. Qwerty nearly dropped the bowl of cornflakes he was holding. "We gotta get him out of here," Qwerty said solemnly.

"That's what I've been trying to tell you!" replied Joey.

"Why do you think he took his clothes off?"

"How should I know? Maybe he was hot."

"He's awfully . . . flabby," Qwerty said, walking around Franklin.

"It looks like he's wearing a skin suit."

"Does this mean we're going to look like this when we're old?"

"Man, I hope not."

Franklin opened his eyes and looked around as if there was nothing unusual about the situation. "It seems my fate constantly to wish for repose and never to obtain it," he said.

"Uh, Mr. Franklin," Qwerty asked. "What are you doing?"

"Taking an air bath," the old man replied matter-of-factly.

"With no clothes on?" Joey asked.

"That, my young friend, is precisely what makes it an air bath!"

"Jeez!" Qwerty exclaimed. "Can't you put on a towel or something? Nobody wants to see you naked. I mean, this is my *house!*"

"I've never heard of an air bath," said Joey, who knew just about everything about history.

"This practice is not in the least painful," Franklin explained as he began putting his clothes back on, "but on the contrary, agreeable and preserving of health. If I return to my bedchamber afterward, I make a supplement to my night's rest of one or two hours of the most pleasing sleep that can be imagined."

"Mr. Franklin, I think it's time we get you home," Qwerty said.

"I suppose I must," Franklin agreed. "There are pressing matters I must attend to in Philadelphia."

Qwerty handed Franklin the bowl of cereal and went to fiddle with the computer as he munched a Pop-Tart. Franklin examined the food cautiously, sniffing it. "What, may I ask, is this?"

"Cornflakes," Joey replied.

"But there is little resemblance to corn as I know it."

"They grind it up or something," Joey replied. "Then they make it into flakes."

"Just eat it," Qwerty said as he snapped a photo of Franklin's face with his digital camera.

"Mmmm, crunchy!" Franklin said, scooping a second spoonful. "Yet the taste of corn is curiously absent."

Qwerty popped the disk out of the camera and slipped it into his computer. With a few mouse clicks, Benjamin Franklin's face appeared seconds later on the computer screen. Photography was not invented until 1826, and the last time a portrait had been made of him, Franklin had sat still for hours as an artist painted it. His head snapped back with surprise.

"It's a digital picture," Qwerty explained. "I transmitted it from the camera into the computer. Then I'll go to the Virtual Tour of Philadelphia Web site and use the Anytime Anywhere Machine to zap you back to seventeen seventy-six."

Qwerty might as well have been speaking Chinese. But Franklin was doing his best to follow what the boy was saying.

"Basically," added Joey, "he's going to reverse the process he used to bring you here in the first place."

"Extraordinary!" exclaimed Franklin, finishing off the cornflakes.

"It's really quite simple," Qwerty said.

Joey flipped the switch on the Anytime Anywhere Machine, which Qwerty had hidden in a box under his bed to prevent his little sister from fooling with it. Franklin watched curiously as Qwerty logged on, clicked the mysterious buttons, and typed a bewildering series of commands into the keyboard. One of the most famous scientists of his day, Franklin could only dimly comprehend what was about to happen to him.

"Okay," Qwerty said excitedly, "when I hit the ENTER key, you'll be instantly transported back to July fourth, seventeen seventy-six. Are you ready?"

"Commence the voyage, my young captain Elvis. It has been my pleasure making your acquaintance. If you should find yourself in the colony of Pennsylvania in seventeen seventy-six, I sincerely hope you will visit my humble abode so I might treat you to the same gracious hospitality you have shown to me."

"Good luck with the revolution," Qwerty said, his finger on the mouse button, ready to click Franklin back more than two hundred years.

"Wait!" Joey shouted abruptly.

"What?" Qwerty asked, alarmed.

"I just thought of something."

Joey paused for a moment, to make certain he really wanted to say what he was about to say. "Send me with him."

"What?"

"I want to go with Mr. Franklin," Joey decided calmly. "I want to be a witness to history."

"No way!" Qwerty exclaimed. "You're out of your mind!"

"You can do it, Qwerty! Just shoot my picture and scan it in. You said yourself it was simple."

"Your company would be a delight," Franklin told Joey.

"It's insane!" Qwerty insisted. "The revolution took years, didn't it? You'd miss school. And if I sent you back, your dad would totally freak out. You'd be grounded for life, if you lived that long."

"Qwerty," Joey took the seat next to his friend and whispered in his ear, "you're going to send him to Philadelphia on July fourth, seventeen seventy-six. You know what happened on July fourth, seventeen seventy-six, don't you? The Declaration of Independence was signed on that day! It was, like, the most important day in American history! It was the day we declared ourselves to be separate from England!"

"So?"

"Just send me back for a few hours," Joey pleaded. "I want to see what happened, with my own eyes. You can bring me back at dinnertime. My dad is working late tonight. Nobody will ever know I was gone except for you."

Qwerty thought about his friend's proposal.

Technically, it could work. What harm could be done?

"All right," Qwerty finally agreed. "I'll do it, but on one condition."

"What?"

"I'm going to go with you."

"Why?" Joey asked. "You're not interested in history. You only care about *new* stuff. Computers, electronics—"

"You're my best friend," Qwerty explained. "I couldn't let you do this by yourself. It's too dangerous."

"I would be delighted to entertain both of you fine young men," said Franklin, turning away from the globe on Qwerty's desk.

"Besides," Qwerty told Joey, "I'm not gonna let you get all the extra credit!"

"Let's rock and roll, Q-Man!"

Qwerty took a digital photo of Joey, then passed the camera over to Joey to shoot one of him. He zapped both images into the computer and positioned them on the screen next to the photo he had taken of Benjamin Franklin.

"Are you ready?" Qwerty asked.

"Ready," Joey said, gripping the armrest of his chair as if he were on a roller coaster.

"Ready," Franklin said.

Qwerty gave them the thumbs-up sign and pushed the ENTER key. Instantly, Qwerty, Joey, and Benjamin Franklin vanished from West Orange and the twenty-first century.

Unfortunately, Qwerty forgot one small detail. How would they ever get back?

5

Truly a Disturbed Individual

As Qwerty Stevens was pressing the ENTER key on his computer, Ashley Quadrel was in his car, driving over to Qwerty Stevens's house.

Ashley Quadrel was a short, odd-looking man. His eyes, for some reason, were unusually close together. When he looked somebody in the eye, that person never quite had the feeling that they were looking at each other. It was almost as though Quadrel couldn't decide if he should look at your left eye or your right eye. So it appeared as though he were looking right through you.

Other people collected coins or stamps or PEZ dispensers. Ashley Quadrel collected two-dollar bills. Whenever he got some money, he would go to the bank and cash it in for two-dollar bills. He seemed to enjoy having something that nobody else had.

Ashley Quadrel, was, in a word, a loser. He had failed at just about everything he had attempted in his life. He had been a poor student. In high school he had tried out for just about every sport, but no coach wanted him on a team. He'd never had a girlfriend, as women found him weird and unattractive. He loved music and tried to get into several rock bands, but he could never figure out how to play any musical instruments. Now in his mid-thirties, he was too old to be a rock star, anyway.

Quadrel had high hopes of becoming an inventor, and was convinced he was a genius like Thomas Edison. Watching TV one day, he noticed that his remote control was out of his reach. A brainstorm came to his head—what if he invented a *second* remote control that he could use to control the *first* remote control? Then he wouldn't have to get up off his couch to pick up the first remote control! I'm *brilliant!* he thought.

Quadrel actually built such a device, and tried to get some high-tech companies interested in manufacturing it. He had no success at all. Several of the people he approached laughed in his face.

He lived with his mother in a cheap apartment, furnished with things he had picked out of the garbage and decorated mostly with things he had stolen. One thing that Ashley Quadrel *was* good at was stealing.

Usually dressed in a ratty flannel shirt and jeans, he looked like a short, tubby lumberjack. But Ashley Quadrel had never wielded an ax or worked with his hands. In fact, he had hardly ever worked at all. At least not the kind of work most adults did to earn a living.

The only job Ashley Quadrel ever held for more than a few weeks was a year-long stint as a researcher for The Sixth Sense Institute in Livingston, New Jersey. The Sixth Sense was a nonprofit organization that attempted to prove the existence of paranormal phenomena—UFOs, Bigfoot, alien abductions, extrasensory perception, and so on.

It was the perfect job for Ashley Quadrel. Having dropped out of high school and pretty much rejected the whole notion of formal education, Quadrel would tend to believe whatever anyone told him. If somebody told him his next-door neighbor knew the guy who *really* assassinated President Kennedy, Quadrel would accept that as the truth. If somebody told him that dolphins could communicate with humans telepathically, or that visitors from other planets lived among us disguised as humans, that was evidence enough for Ashley Quadrel.

Rumors had been floating around The Sixth Sense Institute—and in scientific circles—that Thomas Edison had created a secret invention that he had never told anyone about. The great inventor had patented over a thousand inventions in his lifetime, but *this* one was supposedly "different."

Some people said it was a device that would allow living people to communicate with the dead. Others claimed it was a perpetual-motion machine, or some kind of anti-aging gizmo. People from all over the world would gather in Internet chat rooms to debate and discuss this mysterious device that Edison (who died in 1931) had refused to share with the world. Some of them were nutcases like Ashley Quadrel; others were skeptics. All were intrigued.

Ashley Quadrel was quite sure there *was* a secret Edison invention hidden somewhere. And if there was such a machine, Edison must have done something with it before he died. And because Quadrel lived just a few miles from Edison's old laboratory in West Orange, he decided he was in the perfect position to find the machine.

If he could find it, he could possess its powers.

After Edison died, the laboratory became a museum—the Edison National Historic Site— which it remains to this day. Quadrel did a lot of poking around there, asking questions, requesting information. He was dismissed as a harmless crackpot.

Then one night a security guard caught Quadrel with a shovel digging holes in the ground behind the laboratory. The police were called, and he was arrested for trespassing and destroying government property.

Getting arrested and having to pay a fine did not stop him. Ashley Quadrel was obsessed with the idea of a secret Edison invention. He went to Llewellyn Park, the site of Edison's home, which was just down the road from the laboratory. He went door to door questioning the people who lived in the neighborhood.

"Did you ever find any unusual machine in your house when you moved in?" he would ask.

"Do you know anybody who ever mentioned such a machine?"

That was how Ashley Quadrel first encountered Qwerty Stevens.

Most of the people Quadrel questioned simply told him they'd never heard of such a machine and sent him on his way. But this Stevens kid with the weird first name was evasive. He looked nervous. He and his big sister looked like they had something to hide. When they said "No," they looked like they were lying.

Which, of course, they *were*. Qwerty had dug up the Anytime Anywhere Machine from his backyard the day before Quadrel had come snooping around.

In some respects, you could say that Ashley Quadrel was a stupid man. But in some respects he was quite bright. He knew Qwerty had the Anytime Anywhere Machine, and he knew what could be done with it.

Ashley Quadrel desperately wanted to get his hands on this machine.

He would lie in bed at night and—in his sick mind—imagine what he would do if he had the Anytime Anywhere Machine. He would go to Egypt in the time of King Tutankhamen and steal all his treasures. He would go to Washington in 1865 and become a national hero by preventing the assassination of President Lincoln. He would go back to 1956, kidnap Elvis Presley, and impersonate him for the rest of his life.

Ashley Quadrel was truly a disturbed individual.

To achieve his twisted goals, Quadrel would have to steal the Anytime Anywhere Machine from Qwerty Stevens. So he began spying on the boy. He would park his car—a battered old Volkswagon Beetle—down the street from Qwerty's house and sit there for hours watching. In a little notebook he would record what time the children went to school each morning, what time the parents left for work, what time the family returned home at night, and what days the cleaning lady showed up. None of the Stevens family suspected a thing.

It did not take long for Quadrel to figure out exactly when the house was empty. He was ready to make his move. He had no idea Qwerty would leave school early on this particular day.

If not for a traffic jam, Ashley Quadrel would have arrived at Qwerty Stevens's house while Benjamin Franklin was still in the boy's bedroom. But thanks to a three-car pileup on Route 280, he was delayed by ten minutes. When he pulled his car up to the curb two blocks away from the Stevens residence, nobody was home. He pulled a large trash bag out of his trunk. This is what he planned to use to conceal the Anytime Anywhere Machine.

Ashley Quadrel was a failure at most of the things he attempted. But he did have two talents: stealing, of course, and climbing. He could climb just about anything. If there was the tiniest hole or crack in a wall to dig a toe or hand into, Quadrel could climb that wall. Even as a child, Ashley Quadrel could outclimb every kid in his school.

After ringing the front doorbell just to make sure nobody was home, Quadrel walked around to the side of the house, where Qwerty's second-floor bedroom was. There was a drainpipe extending down from the roof. Quadrel shimmied up the pipe. When he got to Qwerty's window—the one with the basketball stickers on it—he reached over. He smiled when he saw that the window was not locked from the inside.

The Anytime Anywhere Machine is as good as mine, he thought as he lifted the window.

6

The True Author

The teachers at Thomas Edison Middle School did not get a lot of free time during the school day. Most of the teachers would spend their lunch hour gabbing with one another in the teachers' lounge. Miss Vera Vaughn, by far the oldest teacher in the school, didn't have much in common with her colleagues. She hadn't seen the latest movies or watched the hottest new TV shows. They didn't interest her.

Miss Vaughn usually ate lunch in her classroom while her students were in the cafeteria. She liked the quiet, and she welcomed the chance to grade tests, read assignments, or prepare her lesson plans. That way, she would not have to bring work home with her at the end of the day.

As she picked at a salad, she pulled out her file labeled AMERICAN REVOLUTION REPORTS.

Some of the students' papers were truly pathetic. It was obvious which ones put a lot of work into his or her assignment and which ones just dashed something off without caring how it turned out. Matt Mehorter's paper was three pages of scrawled words that Miss Vaughn could barely decipher. She gave him a C minus even though he deserved a D. The boy had seen so much failure in his life that she felt a little sorry for him. "Try harder!" she wrote at the top of the page.

Miss Vaughn smiled when she picked up Joey Dvorak's paper. Nice and neat. Well organized. Thoughtful. *If only all my students cared so much.* She sighed. She gave Joey an A plus, and wrote the word "Excellent!" with a red pen.

Qwerty's report was the next one on the pile. Miss Vaughn was never sure with Qwerty. Sometimes he turned in brilliant work that showed a lot of effort. Other times, he would forget to do the assignment entirely. She knew he had a mild learning disability, and tried to be sensitive about that when dealing with the boy.

Her first reaction when she riffled through the pages was that Qwerty did a terrific job. There were twelve pages that were computer-printed, with nice artwork neatly surrounded by the text, and no obvious spelling errors. *Perhaps Qwerty is finally getting his act together,* Miss Vaughn thought. With this kind of work plus the fact that Qwerty had brought that Benjamin Franklin impersonator to school, she was prepared to give the boy extra credit.

But as she read the first few sentences of Qwerty's report, she realized almost immediately that something was wrong. The writing was too good, for one thing. It didn't sound as if it had been written by a seventh grader. It certainly didn't sound as if it was written by Qwerty Stevens.

Miss Vaughn continued reading. After two more sentences her eyebrows raised up, and then narrowed down. Two sentences after that, her mouth dropped open. That was when Miss Vaughn realized exactly who the true author of the paper was.

It was Miss Vera Vaughn.

7

Big Trouble

Once he climbed inside Qwerty Stevens's window, Ashley Quadrel looked around and muttered, "What a mess!"

Quadrel, to his credit, was a very neat person. In *his* room at his mother's house, everything was always in its place. The stolen artwork on his walls was framed and perfectly lined up. Everything he owned was junk, but his junk was carefully labeled and organized. He knew exactly how many pairs of socks and underwear were in his drawer and how many were in the wash. His neatness and organizational skills made his mother very happy.

She had no idea they were also symptoms of her son's mental instability.

Quadrel searched Qwerty's room until he finally found the crude wooden box hidden under the bed. He opened it, chuckling to himself that the silly boy hadn't even had the sense to close the lock on it. He laughed to himself when he read the note Qwerty had left inside.

To whom it may concern . . .

The machine inside this box is a secret machine. It is the only one of its kind in the world. It is a very powerful machine. If it fell into the wrong hands, there's no telling what might happen . . .

Here, at last, was the marvelous machine he had obsessed over! It was a beautiful and mysterious thing, a jumble of wires and magnets and relays and switches. Only Edison knew how it worked, and he was long dead.

No matter. You didn't have to know how a car worked to drive one. You didn't have to know how a clock worked to tell time.

Two wires extended out the back of the

Anytime Anywhere Machine. Quadrel followed them under the bed and up the desk to the back of Qwerty's computer.

Ashley Quadrel knew his way around a personal computer quite well. He had learned on state-of-the-art equipment while he was working at The Sixth Sense. But he had been fired from that job and couldn't go back there. His computer at home was an obsolete, older model he had picked up for ten dollars at a yard sale. There was no way he would be able to hook that computer up to the Anytime Anywhere Machine. He had no trusted friends who would let him use their computer.

He cursed to himself. This was a problem.

For a brief moment, Quadrel considered stealing Qwerty's computer along with Edison's machine. Nah, he thought. He'd have to take the monitor, the scanner, and the computer itself and sneak the whole system out of the house and down the street to his car. Too risky.

Quadrel sat at Qwerty's desk to think things over. How could he get the machine out of the boy's room and hook it up with a computer to use it for his own devious purposes?

Quadrel's arm brushed against the computer mouse, which caused the screen saver—an army of flying toasters—to vanish. On the screen was a virtual tour of Philadelphia on July fourth, seventeen seventy-six. On one side of the screen were digital photos of Qwerty, Joey, and Benjamin Franklin.

"What have we *here?*" Quadrel mumbled to himself.

For the time being, Ashley Quadrel forgot about his scheme to steal the Anytime Anywhere Machine. There was a perfectly good computer right here. Everything was all hooked up and ready to go. Nobody was home.

At that moment, the phone on Qwerty's desk rang. Ashley Quadrel looked at it for a moment. The smart thing to do would be to ignore it. But Quadrel, more often than not, did not do the smart thing. "Whaddaya want?" he asked upon picking up the phone.

"Who is this?" asked Miss Vera Vaughn, who knew immediately that the voice on the phone did not belong to Qwerty's father. "Is this Mr. Franklin?"

"Huh?" asked Ashley Quadrel, glancing up at Benjamin Franklin's picture on the computer screen.

"I mean, is this the man who was impersonating Benjamin Franklin at school this morning?"

"Who wants to know?"

"This is Miss Vaughn, Qwerty's social studies teacher. May I speak with Qwerty please? I have something very important that I must discuss with him."

"Is he in trouble?"

"He is in very big trouble," Miss Vaughn said. "He copied an article about the American Revolution from the Internet for his report that he turned in this morning. That is a very serious offense."

"How do you know he copied it?"

"Because I am the author of the article!" Miss Vaughn said. "I wrote it under a pen name. Qwerty plagiarized it from the Web site!"

Ashley Quadrel chuckled to himself. "Well, he ain't here," he said.

Miss Vaughn, already disturbed because Qwerty had plagiarized the paper, was doubly upset. The man on the telephone, she realized, couldn't be the same charming man she had met at school. A Benjamin Franklin impersonator would never use the word *ain't*.

"Who *is* this?" she demanded.

"That's for me to know and you to find out," Ashley Quadrel said.

"Well, is he coming back to school this afternoon?" Miss Vaughn asked. But Quadrel had already hung up the phone. Miss Vaughn quickly dialed the number at Joey Dvorak's house, but there was no answer.

Ashley Quadrel looked at the computer screen with the July 4, 1776 Web site and the photos of the boys alongside Benjamin Franklin's photo.

"It looks like my little oddly named friend is playing hookey in Philadelphia," Quadrel muttered, taking the mouse in his hand.

Despite his lack of formal education, Ashley Quadrel knew that the Declaration of Independence—perhaps the most famous and treasured document in American history—had been signed on July 4, 1776. Most Americans knew that.

A smile spread slowly across his face as an illegal, immoral, and utterly insane thought came into Ashley Quadrel's mind: The Declaration of Independence would look *perfect* on his bedroom wall.

8

The House of Yesterday

A millisecond or two after Qwerty Stevens had tapped the ENTER key on his computer, the Anytime Anywhere Machine went into action.

Using a technological secret that Thomas Edison took with him to his grave, the machine deconstructed Qwerty, Joey, and Benjamin Franklin molecule-by-molecule. A few milliseconds later, the trio was reconstructed in Philadelphia at 2:13 P.M. on July 4, 1776. It would be another fifteen minutes until Ashley Quadrel would shimmy up the drainpipe on Qwerty's house.

"Ouch!"

Joey landed so close to a roaring fireplace that he burned his fingers. Qwerty and Franklin landed a few feet away on a rug.

"Where are we?" Qwerty asked groggily.

"Welcome to my home!" Franklin said as he dusted off his vest. "That machine of yours works with rather remarkable accuracy!"

"We did it!" Joey marveled, forgetting his burned fingers.

The room they were in was Franklin's kitchen, but it was unlike any kitchen Qwerty or Joey had ever seen. There was no refrigerator, gas stove, or other appliances, of course. There was no sink, no running water. The huge fireplace, with a chimney extending up from it, was obviously used for all the cooking. There was a big pot in the fire. Something was cooking in the pot, and it smelled delicious.

In the corner of the room was a circular pit— about four feet wide and ten feet down—that was used to keep fruits and vegetables cold.

Qwerty unbuttoned the top button of his shirt. It was an extremely hot day, and the crackling fire pushed the room temperature over a hundred degrees. Flies buzzed around noisily. Qwerty thought about asking Franklin to turn on the air conditioner, but the first air conditioner wouldn't be turned on until 1902.

Two walls of the kitchen were brick, the other two plaster with patterned wallpaper. Framed portraits hung on the walls, along with cooking utensils and knickknacks. A grandfather clock ticked loudly in the corner. The room was dark for a sunny afternoon. The fire provided a little light, and so did two small windows.

Qwerty got up off the floor to look out the window, but his eye was caught by the glass itself. It wasn't perfectly smooth, like the glass he was used to. Faint ripples made the image wavy.

"May I have the pleasure of escorting you gentlemen on a tour?" Franklin asked.

Using his cane for support, the old man walked the boys through three floors of rooms that looked—to them—much like a museum. Just about everything was made from wood. Candlesticks and whale-oil lanterns were mounted on the walls.

"What's that?" Joey asked every time he saw something he had never seen before.

"Merely a chair," Franklin replied. He sat down and began to slowly pump a foot pedal at the bottom, which caused a fan to rotate and blow air on Franklin's head. "It lowers the temperature, and also keeps flies away."

"Cool!" Qwerty said.

"What's that?" Joey asked in Franklin's library.

"I call that my long arm," Franklin replied, picking up an eight-foot wooden pole with a mechanism of some sort attached to it. He held the pole up to a shelf high above his head. When he squeezed the handle, the end of the pole clasped a book, and Franklin brought it down. "I am too old to be climbing ladders," Franklin explained.

"Cool!" Qwerty said.

"What's this?" Joey asked in Franklin's bedroom.

"Pull it," Franklin said.

Joey pulled on a wooden handle that was dangling from a rope that hung down over the bed. The rope was strung through a pulley system that ran across the ceiling to the bedroom door. When Joey pulled on the rope, the door shut and a lock fell into place.

"I detest leaving a warm bed on a cold night," Franklin said.

"Cool!" Qwerty said, "It's like a remote control."

"I need one of those," Joey said, laughing.

"I may not possess anything quite as marvelous as your computer," chuckled Franklin, "but everything serves its purpose." He clearly enjoyed showing the boys his inventions.

On a shelf in Franklin's bedroom, Joey noticed a large jar. When he looked at it closely, he saw a dead snake inside, floating in water. The snake, incredibly, had two heads and one body.

"One head desired to go to the pond," Franklin explained, "and the other desired to go to the river. Sadly, the snake could not make up its mind and died from thirst. It is the same with people sometimes."

As they toured the house, Qwerty was on the lookout for the bathroom. It wasn't an emergency, but he did have to go. Finally, when the tour seemed to be at its end, Qwerty had no choice but to ask his host, "Can I use your bathroom?"

Franklin stared at him, puzzled.

"You know . . ." Qwerty tried to explain. "I've got to go . . . to the bathroom."

"You desire to bathe?" Franklin asked.

"The john," Joey suggested. "He needs to use the . . . facilities. You know, the rest room."

"Oh!" Franklin finally brightened. "You want

to use the *necessary*. By all means. You will find it out back."

Connected to the back of the house was a little shack that looked like the kind of shed that somebody would store their lawnmower in. As soon as Qwerty stepped inside the dark room, he was hit with a stench that caused him to wrinkle up his nose with disgust. He looked down and saw his feet were about three inches away from the edge of a large, circular, brick-lined pit. One more step and he would have fallen into a month's worth of human waste.

"Ugh!" Qwerty grimaced. Holding his nose with one hand, he did his business and got out of there as fast as he could.

Still retching from the smell, Qwerty returned to Benjamin Franklin's home. No sooner had he walked in the back door than a woman rushed in the front door.

She looked to be about forty—Qwerty's mother's age. Despite the heat, she was encased in several layers of ruffled dresses that reached the floor, a petticoat, and an apron. On her head was a white cotton hat that tied below her chin. "Where have you been?" she asked, hugging Franklin while ignoring the boys. "I was worried to death!"

"Is this your wife?" Joey asked.

"My dear Deborah passed on but two years ago," Franklin said, still hugging the woman. "This is my daughter, Sally."

Sally Franklin let go of her father and bowed to the boys.

"I'm Joey. Pleased to meet you, ma'am."

"I'm Qwerty. You can call me Elvis."

Sally had never seen young men like this before. They were dressed so strangely that for the moment she forgot to greet them politely. "What is on your feet?" she asked.

Qwerty and Joey looked down. "Sneakers," Qwerty replied.

"Perhaps for sneaking around," Franklin explained. "My young friends have different customs where they come from."

Sally didn't press for more information. Her father was one of the most famous men in the world, and he frequently brought unusual visitors home with him. Besides, she had other things on her mind. Sally handed Franklin an envelope. "It is from William," she said simply.

Franklin sighed as he broke the wax seal of the envelope. The joyfulness had left his eyes. He read the letter silently. Grimacing, he crumpled up the letter and threw it into the fire. A tear rolled down Sally's cheek.

"Who is William?" Joey asked.

"My son," Franklin said sadly. "The royal governor of your colony, New Jersey. We were once very close. We no longer speak. He is dead to me now."

"Why?" Qwerty asked.

"William is a Tory," Sally explained. "He remains loyal to King George III. Nothing my father says will cause him to change his mind."

"Isn't loyalty a *good* thing?" Qwerty asked.

"Loyalty is perhaps the most treasured human quality," said Franklin. "But not blind loyalty. If you make yourself a sheep, the wolves will eat you. I fear William has made himself a sheep."

"What did the letter say?" Joey asked.

"William has requested once again that I support the king," Franklin said. "A king who sends his soldiers to these shores to kill innocent people, burn our houses, impose unfair taxes—"

"Father," Sally interrupted, putting a hand on his shoulder.

"My son has broken my heart," Franklin said heavily. "When he chose the king as his master, he lost me as his father."

A loud rapping was heard on the front door,

and Sally hurried over to open it. A teenage boy stood in the doorway. "The presence of Dr. Franklin is requested at the statehouse," he said, slightly out of breath.

"Let us avoid trifling conversation," Franklin said, snapping out of his funk. "I must go."

"Will your young friends be joining us for dinner this evening, Father?"

"I would be delighted if you would accompany us," Franklin told the boys.

"What are you having?" Joey asked, enjoying the smell that was wafting over from the fireplace.

"Squirrel stew," Sally replied.

"Ummmm," Franklin moaned.

"No thanks," Qwerty and Joey replied together.

"As you wish," said Franklin, shuffling toward the door. "Should anyone require my services, I will be at the statehouse."

"Wait!" Joey exclaimed. "Can I come, too?"

"Yeah," Qwerty added, not wanting to be left behind. "We want to come with you."

Franklin fixed his gaze on the boys as Sally went off to do her chores. Joey was determined to follow Franklin whether the old man allowed it or not. He hadn't traveled to July 4, 1776, just to sit in Benjamin Franklin's house.

"Our discussions at the statehouse are quite dull and tedious," Franklin warned.

"I don't care," Joey said. "I want to be there."

"I am not at all certain that you will be admitted."

"Let's try," Qwerty suggested.

"Agreed," Franklin replied. "But first you must put on some proper clothing."

The boys didn't object. If they were to step outside in their twenty-first-century clothing, they would look like a couple of freaks. Franklin's grandson, Temple, was thirteen years old and had a closet full of clothes. Temple was away visiting his father. With Franklin's help, Qwerty and Joey searched through his clothes until they found shirts, vests, frocks, and breeches—pants that ended at the knee—that fit. Soon they looked like real colonial boys.

"Wait a minute," Qwerty protested. "I'm not putting on *tights!*"

"They're not tights, doofus," Joey said as he put them on. "They're *leggings.*"

"Well, okay then," Qwerty agreed reluctantly. "If anybody at school ever saw me dressed like this, I'd have to get plastic surgery or leave town or something."

Franklin handed each of the boys a pair of Temple's shoes, which like most shoes of the colonial period were not specifically made for a left or a right foot. Qwerty examined the shoes carefully before putting them on. "Do I have these on the wrong feet?" he asked.

"Only if you possess another pair of legs," Franklin joked.

Joey got dressed first and was anxious to go. Putting on the ridiculous-looking colonial clothing didn't bother him one bit. He wanted to see history. "Is the Declaration of Independence finished?" he asked Franklin excitedly. "Have you seen it? Will the Liberty Bell be rung?"

"Hold your tongue," Franklin said as he led the boys out the door. "The greatest talkers are the least doers."

9

The United States of Quadreland

While Benjamin Franklin led the boys into the streets of Philadelphia, Ashley Quadrel was sitting at Qwerty's desk in West Orange, psychotic thoughts dancing in his brain.

He would steal the Declaration of Independence, of course, and put it up on the wall of his bedroom next to the framed two-dollar bill—the first thing he had ever stolen. That would be easy.

But why stop there?

His own parents had been born in England, it occurred to Quadrel. Technically, that made him British. Besides stealing the Declaration of Independence, he could *rewrite* it! That's it! He would force the Founding Fathers to turn the Declaration of Independence into a Declaration of Loyalty to the king! If the colonies never declared their independence, America would remain a part of England! Then he could return to the twenty-first century with the knowledge that he had changed history! What a glorious day it would be for the British Empire!

Hail Britannia!

Quadrel pulled a two-dollar bill out of his pocket. The face of Thomas Jefferson was on the front. He turned the bill over and smiled a wicked smile. When they signed the Declaration, the Founding Fathers of America were all in one room at one time. If he could get into that room, he could . . .

KIDNAP GEORGE WASHINGTON!

That's it! He would rewrite the Declaration, steal it, and kidnap the man who would become "the Father of Our Country." Without Washington, there would *be* no country! He, Ashley Quadrel, would be the father of the country! For he, alone, had prevented the American colonies from breaking away from Mother England! He would win the Revolutionary War without firing a shot! Perhaps in gratitude, King George would knight him! Maybe the king would even rename America "Quadreland."

Needless to say, Ashley Quadrel was a sick, sick man.

Before he could obliterate the United States of America from the globe, Quadrel needed to get himself to Philadelphia on July 4, 1776. He knew how to work the Anytime Anywhere Machine, having already transported himself to a confrontation with Thomas Edison in 1879.

As he looked at Qwerty Stevens's monitor he thought about how unfair it was that this *kid* had such a state-of-the-art computer while he—a true genius—had to make do with an obsolete yard-sale piece of junk. Someday, when he was the king of Quadreland, he would right that wrong.

The digital camera was sitting on Qwerty's desk next to the computer. Quadrel turned it on and held it out at arm's length so he could snap his own picture. It wasn't the most flattering photo ever taken of him, but it would do.

He was about to transmit the image into the computer when he noticed there wasn't enough room on the screen. Qwerty, his friend, and Benjamin Franklin took up too much space. Quadrel deleted Franklin's face and put his own in its place.

Now he was ready. Quadrel looked out the bedroom window and smirked. He would leave this wretched modern world—a world that had been so cruel to him—and travel back to a simpler world. It would be a world with no computers, no television, no airplanes, no atomic weapons. Knowing what he knew, he would turn that world upside down.

Quadrel's fantasy was interrupted by the ring of the doorbell downstairs. Miss Vera Vaughn was standing on the front steps.

Fiddling with the buttons on her jacket, Miss Vaughn rang the doorbell a second time and knocked on the door. She had become concerned after the strange conversation with the man on the phone. After getting one of the other teachers to cover her class, she decided to walk over to Qwerty's house to see if he was okay. "Qwerty!" she called, ringing the bell a third time. "Qwerty, are you there?"

Upstairs, Ashley Quadrel was in a panic. What if it was the boy's parents coming home early from work? What if it was the police? He had to get out of there, and there was only one safe exit.

Ashley Quadrel tapped the ENTER key on Qwerty's computer, and vanished.

10

The City of Brotherly Love

Ten minutes before Ashley Quadrel zapped himself to 1776, Qwerty, Joey, and Benjamin Franklin stepped out of Franklin's front door on Market Street. It took a few moments for their eyes to adjust to the bright light of day.

In 1776, Philadelphia was the largest city in America. In fact, it was one of the largest cities in the entire British empire.

The first thing Qwerty and Joey noticed was the *smell*. It was a pungent mixture of cooking food, baking bread, rotting garbage, and manure. People threw their trash right into the cobblestoned streets.

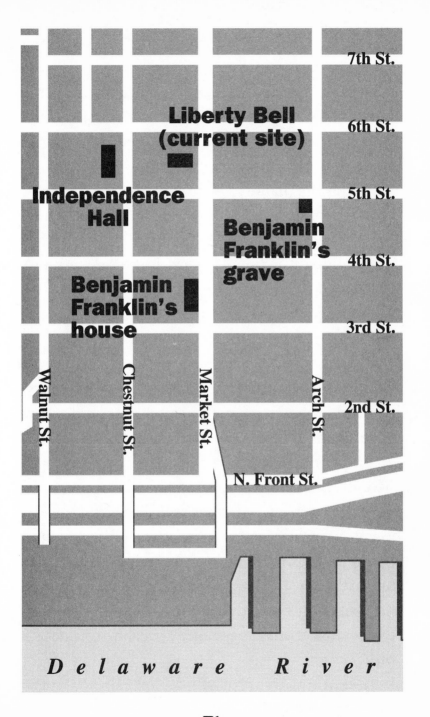

7th St.

Liberty Bell (current site)

6th St.

5th St.

Independence Hall

Benjamin Franklin's grave

4th St.

Benjamin Franklin's house

3rd St.

Walnut St.

Chestnut St.

Market St.

Arch St.

2nd St.

N. Front St.

Delaware River

Pigs wandered from house to house, rooting around until they found something to eat. Smoke hung in the air from the wood and coal stoves that burned in every house despite the hot July day. Horses were everywhere, some pulling buggies and others with riders.

"Mind the manure," Franklin advised the boys.

After side-stepping the mess in the street, Qwerty looked up, expecting to see the Philadelphia "skyline." There was none. Almost all buildings were three stories or less. A few church steeples poked up into the sky. All the buildings were made from wood or brick.

Benjamin Franklin lived in a courtyard off Market Street between Third and Fourth Streets, just a few blocks from the statehouse and a few more from the Delaware River. The masts from tall ships in the busy harbor could be seen from the entrance to the courtyard.

Market Street—which is still the main street of downtown Philly today—had clearly been named for a reason. It was a wide, unpaved boulevard that ran east to west from the river, and was lined with little shops of every description.

Shoemaker . . . rope maker . . . cabinetmaker . . .

tailor . . . glassblower . . . mason . . . blacksmith . . . carpenter . . . clock maker. And taverns. *Lots* of taverns. On the street, everyone was buying, selling, or trading something with somebody else. A vendor sold live chickens from a cart. German, Dutch, Irish, Scotch, African, and British accents could all be heard.

"It's like a mall," Qwerty whispered to Joey, "but outside."

The boys passed by shops they didn't know existed. A "cooper," they learned, made wooden barrels and buckets. The "apothecary" was a drugstore. The window of the "stationers" displayed everything from pencils to soap to cheese.

An old man wheeled a wooden contraption in front of him that had several wheels, pulleys, and a foot pedal. He stopped, pulled out a long knife, and sharpened it on the spinning wheel, sparks flying. A younger man had two long L-shaped strips of wood strapped to his back. The boys watched as a woman handed him some coins to carry a large wooden box down the street for her.

Qwerty and Joey, even dressed in colonial garb, felt as out of place in the eighteenth century as

Franklin must have felt in the twenty-first. They couldn't help but stare as Franklin led them down the busy street.

It was easy to tell the rich from the poor. Rich people ("gentlefolk") were decked out in bright scarlet and crimson suits and petticoats with gold lace and ruffled shirts. Most wore shoes that buckled, and some wore capes. Women's dresses reached the ground.

The poor ("simple folk") wore plain breeches, vests, long smock-like shirts that were brown, gray, pale yellow, or brick red. Some wore moccasins. Many of the people were African-American, and it occurred to Joey that some of them had to be slaves. Slavery would be a part of America for another ninety years.

Everyone wore something on their head. Hats were three-cornered, or straw, or felt with broad brims. Some people wore a turban. Women had woolen caps or a kerchief knotted at the top of the head. Not a baseball cap was in sight. Baseball would not become an organized game until 1845.

Some of the men, to Qwerty's surprise, were obviously wearing wigs. These weren't toupees to cover their baldness. They were full, white, elaborately curled wigs. It was hard not to snicker when a gust of wind came along and a puff of powder would fly off some guy's head. Some of men who didn't wear a wig had a long ponytail sticking out from under a hat.

"Man, this place looks like one of those reconstructed villages," Qwerty said, "only dirtier."

One thing that both boys noticed was that people were *shorter.* Qwerty felt tall, and Joey towered over most people passing by.

"If you lived in these times," Qwerty told his friend, "you could play in the NBA."

"There *was* no NBA in these times," Joey pointed out.

"No, but they still had the seventy-sixers," Qwerty joked.

Benjamin Franklin, certainly the most famous man in Philadelphia and one of the most famous in the world, was recognized almost as soon as he stepped out of his doorway. Men, women, and children came up to him to shake his hand, clap him on the back, or ask a question.

"Dr. Franklin," they all called him, "are you well? Where are you off to? Meet my son! What words of wisdom have you for us on this fine day?" And so on.

"My deepest regrets," Franklin would reply as

he continued on his way. "I am very late for an important meeting at the statehouse."

"What will the Continental Congress decide?" a woman asked. "Will they vote for independence?"

"I know not."

"Dr. Franklin," a street peddler shouted as he blocked the old man's path. "You who snatched lightning from the heavens. Surely you will appreciate this clever machine I have devised."

The peddler held up a metal gizmo with an apple stuck to the end of it. As he turned a crank at the other end, the apple turned around and a blade came down and sliced the peel off neatly in one long, curly strip.

"Ingenious!" exclaimed the delighted Franklin. He handed the man a bill.

The peddler gave him the machine and allowed Franklin to pass.

"An apple a day keeps the doctor away!" the peddler called out.

As soon as the peddler was gone, Franklin gave the apple peeler to an astonished black man passing by.

"Don't you want it?" Qwerty asked.

"There are hundreds of similar devices available."

"So why did you buy it?"

"Time is money," Franklin said, "and my colleagues await my arrival."

"Wasn't it you who said 'a penny saved is a penny earned'?" Joey asked.

"Yes," Franklin agreed, "but frugality is a virtue I never could acquire in myself."

In Greek, the word *philadelphia* means "brotherly love." But as the trio got within a block of the statehouse, it appeared as though there was very little brotherly love in Philadelphia. Or, at least there was very little on July 4, 1776. The street was teeming with people, and it didn't appear as if they were working or selling anything. Angry voices could be heard in every direction.

"King George is a tyrant!" somebody shouted, waving a fist in the air.

"Independence!" yelled another. "The time has come for America to be free from British rule!"

A tavern sign with a painting of King George III on it was roughly yanked off a building and tossed into a bonfire with other objects that had images of England on them.

"Burn it!" someone screamed. "Destroy even the shadow of that king who refused to reign over a free people!"

Across the street, a dummy of King George III was hanging from a flagpole. A teenage boy draped a British flag over the head and set it on fire with a torch.

"Quickly," Franklin told the boys. "We must hurry. Lost time is never found again."

As they pushed their way through the protesters, Qwerty and Joey overheard whispered rumors that were spreading through the crowd.

"The British are going to set the city on fire!"

"They'll starve us out. That's what they intend to do."

"The French will come to our aid."

"But who will protect us from the French?"

"British tyranny is much preferable to French rule."

For every angry patriot shouting in the street, it seemed like there was somebody else—a loyalist—who supported the policies of King George III and wanted America to continue under British rule.

"Mother England founded these colonies," an older gentleman said. "Has she not the right to rule them as she sees fit?"

"My family is in Britain still," complained his wife. "If we go to war, they will be harmed."

"How do we know an American government will be more fair than our own king?" asked a young man in a dark waistcoat.

"We are, after all, British!" reasoned a plump, red-haired man. A cabbage came flying through the air and narrowly missed hitting him.

The loyalists were—for the most part—quieter and not as angry as the patriots. Change was in the air, and perhaps revolution and war. If the loyalists opposed it vocally, there was no telling what might happen to them when it was all over. Nobody wants to be on the side of a loser.

Besides, there were men marching around with guns.

On the grassy field at Fifth street, the Pennsylvania militia—part-time solders—was drilling. They were a motley bunch of men, some elderly and some not much older than Qwerty and Joey. A few had smart blue uniforms, but most were dressed in street clothes. Each soldier had a shot pouch and a powder horn slung over his shoulder.

In the first row of soldiers was a boy—he couldn't have been older than ten—pounding on a drum that hung around his neck. He could play seven different drumbeats, each one giving the soldiers a specific instruction. A certain drumbeat meant it was time to march. Another drumbeat meant the enemy was approaching.

Little children had gathered around to watch the militia march back and forth across the grass as the leader barked out commands. Joey Dvorak stopped, too. He couldn't resist. He had been fascinated by war since he was a toddler, and he also played drums in the school orchestra. "Look at the size of those muskets!" Joey marveled. "They must be seven feet long, with bayonets!"

A group of men and women had gathered at the edge of the green and were hollering at the soldiers.

"Lay down your guns! Fighting remedies no problem!"

They were Quakers, who took no side in the dispute with England and whose religion centered around nonviolence. Pennsylvania had been founded—and even named—for a Quaker named William Penn. Many of the citizens of Philadelphia followed Quaker doctrines.

Qwerty had to pull Joey away from watching the militia.

The street scene was a confusion of patriots, loyalists, Quakers, angry men and women, bewildered children, and some people who were simply going about their everyday lives and jobs. Of all these people gathered in Philadelphia, only two of them knew what was going to happen: Qwerty Stevens and Joey Dvorak.

"Should we tell 'em how it's all gonna turn out?" Qwerty asked his friend. "Maybe it would ease the tension if they knew we won the war."

Joey thought it over for a moment. "I don't think so," he decided. "Let 'em find out on their own."

Finally they made their way through the crowds until they were standing outside the statehouse. It was a big, redbrick, two-story building, with a center section that towered three floors higher than the rest, and a large clock just below a steeple that came to a point high above the street. Joey stopped once again, this time to look up in wonder. "This is it!" he exclaimed.

"This is *what?*" asked Qwerty.

"Independence Hall! You've seen pictures of it. The Pennsylvania statehouse is the same thing as Independence Hall. They must have renamed it after the revolution."

Joey was absolutely right. He also knew that if

this was Independence Hall, and if it was July 4 of 1776, then fifty-six men were inside making a decision that would rock the world.

"Boys," Franklin said seriously, "we must part company at this time. Will you be able to carry on without my assistance?"

"No way!" Joey said. "We're going in there with you."

"Yeah," Qwerty agreed. "We came *this* far."

"That would be rather impossible," Franklin stammered. "Only representatives of the individual colonies are permitted inside. There is a security—"

"You've got to get us in," Joey insisted, maintaining eye contact with Franklin.

"We got *you* past the security at our school," Qwerty argued.

This was a problem. These boys were quite adamant about getting into the statehouse.

Benjamin Franklin had always been a practical man who got pleasure out of finding solutions to everyday problems. When he observed that lightning was striking buildings and causing them to burn down, he invented the lightning rod to divert the electricity into the ground. When he observed that almost all the heat from a fireplace went up the chimney, he invented a freestanding stove—that became known as the Franklin stove—to spread the heat around the room. When he became weary of having to carry around two pairs of eye glasses to see both near and far, he invented bifocals.

Surely there was a simple solution to this problem, too.

He found it.

Franklin allowed his knees to buckle beneath him and he collapsed in a heap on the dirt outside the statehouse.

"Dr. Franklin!" shouted Joey. "Are you okay?"

"I think he had a heart attack!" Qwerty exclaimed.

Sitting on the ground, Franklin rolled his eyes. "Pick me up, you fools!" he said, giving Joey a gentle whack with the cane. "This is merely a ploy to gain you admittance to the statehouse."

Qwerty and Joey got on either side and hoisted the old man up, which was not easy. He was over two hundred pounds of dead weight.

"What now?" Qwerty said, grimacing.

"Carry me up the stairs," Franklin instructed.

The boys did as they were told. A burly man

with a rifle and a bad case of body odor stood stiffly in front of the door. "Dr. Franklin!" he said. "Your arrival has been anticipated with great expectation."

"Excellent."

The boys were about to carry Franklin inside when the guard blocked the doorway with his rifle. "Who might *you* be?" he asked suspiciously.

"These young men are my servants," Franklin explained. "My gout is troubling me terribly, so they must ferry me about."

"Yeah, we're his servants," Qwerty said, nodding.

"Servants are not permitted inside, Doctor," the burly security guard said, almost apologetically. "None of the other representatives brought servants."

"None of the other representatives have reached their seventieth year!" thundered Franklin.

"He can't walk," Joey added, stating the obvious. After carrying Franklin for a few minutes, it felt like the old man weighed *three* hundred pounds.

"Take me home, boys," Franklin ordered.

"Clearly, the elderly are not welcomed, desired, or necessary in these goings-on."

"Bring him in, for heaven's sake!" called a voice inside the statehouse. The guard stepped aside, and the boys carried Franklin into the hallway.

"Who was that?" Joey asked.

"That," Franklin replied, "was my esteemed colleague from the colony of Virginia, Mr. Thomas Jefferson."

11

The Right Place at the Right Time

About the time Qwerty, Joey, and Benjamin Franklin entered the statehouse, Ashley Quadrel landed with a thud in Benjamin Franklin's kitchen.

"Eeeeeeeeeeeeeeeeek!" shrieked a terrified Sally Franklin, who had been stirring her squirrel stew. "Who the devil are you? Where have you come from?"

"None of your business, sister," Quadrel replied. "I'm here and that's all that matters."

"Please do not hurt me," Sally begged. "I will give you anything you desire."

"Just answer my questions and you won't get hurt," Quadrel demanded. "Am I in Philadelphia?"

"Y-yes."

"Is the year seventeen seventy-six?"

"Yes, of course."

"July fourth, seventeen seventy-six?"

"Yes."

Quadrel pumped his fist triumphantly. For once in his life, he was in the right place at the right time. The right place at the right time to achieve greatness. For once, he hadn't messed things up. "How far am I from Independence Hall?" he demanded.

"I have never heard of such a place," Sally replied honestly. "Are you certain it is in Philadelphia?"

"Don't get smart with me, sister!" Quadrel snapped, taking a step toward Sally. "How can you live in Philadelphia and not know what Independence Hall is?"

"I have no idea—"

"Independence Hall!" the little man shouted, as if repeating it louder would make her understand. "They signed the Declaration of Independence there! The Constitution, too! What are you, stupid in the head?"

"What Constitution?" Sally asked.

Ashley Quadrel was furious. He was getting

nowhere with this imbecile. He paced the room thinking about his next move. He could just go out on his own and find Independence Hall on his own. But he was in a hurry. What if he got lost and missed the signing of the Declaration?

The framed portraits on the walls caught his eye. "Say," he said, "That guy is Benjamin Franklin, isn't he?"

"Why yes, of course. Father sat for that painting not more than a fortnight ago."

"Wait a minute," Quadrel said, a gleam in his eye. "Benjamin Franklin is your *father?* And I'm in Benjamin Franklin's *house?*"

"Certainly," Sally replied, puzzled. *Everyone* knew her father and where he lived. Why was this strange man making such a fuss over it? And why was he dressed so oddly?

Quadrel laughed an evil, cackling laugh that gave Sally the shivers, even though she had never seen a movie with a villian who had an evil, cackling laugh.

This is perfect, Quadrel thought. Benjamin Franklin had to be where the Declaration of Independence was being signed. He would use Franklin's daughter to lead him to Franklin. Everything was falling into place. "Take me to your father!" ordered Quadrel.

"I will not," Sally blustered. "You are a madman!"

Ashley Quadrel had hoped it wouldn't come to this. He hadn't been expecting any resistance, at least not at this stage of the game. But he had to do what he had to do.

He reached into the waistband of his pants and pulled out a Smith & Wesson .44 revolver. He had purchased it illegally from a man he'd met in prison after his first arrest. Quadrel hadn't gone so far as to buy any bullets for the gun yet, but figured the sight of the .44 itself would be enough to frighten people into giving him what he wanted.

"Is that a pistol?" asked Sally, unimpressed. She had never seen a gun like that.

"Of *course* it's a pistol, you idiot!" Quadrel shouted. "And it can blow a hole in your head the size of a Reese's Peanut Butter Cup!"

"What is that?" asked the bewildered Sally.

"Shut up!" Quadrel barked. "Take me to your father, or I'll shoot you. Are you bright enough to understand *that?*"

"Follow me," Sally Franklin simply said, and she led Quadrel out the door to Market Street.

12

The Declaration of Independence

By this time, Qwerty, Joey, and Franklin had stepped through the large wooden door of the statehouse. After allowing them to pass, the guard resumed his post on the outside of the door. Now that Benjamin Franklin had finally arrived, no one else would be admitted to the building.

Franklin instructed the boys to carry him through a hallway and turn left into a much larger room. The one thing that stood out about this room was the fact that it was so *green.*

The walls—bare of any art—were a dullish green. The curtains that covered six big windows were green. Thirteen tables arranged in a wide semicircle around a larger table all had green tablecloths on them.

An ornate chandelier hung from the ceiling. A candlestick had been placed on each of the tables. Two fireplaces mercifully had not been lit. But the windows had been shut and carefully locked to make certain that nobody outside could overhear the conversation. Qwerty wiped his forehead with his sleeve. The temperature inside the room was nearly one hundred degrees.

But to Joey Dvorak, the heat was not a problem. He took little notice of the room or its furnishings. What captured Joey's attention were the people sitting at those tables. Fifty-six representatives from the thirteen original colonies. The Founding Fathers of the United States of America.

There was John Hancock, a tall dandy who stood behind the center table and was presiding over the meeting. He was one of the richest men in America. There was Thomas Jefferson, with flaming red hair, and long legs that made him tower over everyone. He looked to be in a sour mood. There was the pugnacious John Adams, a short, stocky, self-made man from Massachusetts.

"Dr. Franklin," Adams said, a slight sneer on

his face, "it is so kind of you to at long last grace us with your presence."

"I was detained," Franklin said, bowing his head. "Please accept my most sincere apology."

"You were assigned to assist me with my labors," Jefferson said sternly.

"And I shall," said Franklin.

"It is just as well that he is late," snorted Adams. "If Dr. Franklin had written the Declaration of Independence, he would have put jokes in it."

The other delegates erupted into laughter, which broke the tension in the room somewhat. Even Jefferson smiled.

Franklin, still being carried by Qwerty and Joey, pointed to where they could lower him into a chair. The delegates from the northern states were seated at the tables on the left side of the room, and the southern delegates were seated at the right. Seeing that all the chairs were taken, the boys quietly sat on the floor behind Franklin and the other delegates from Pennsylvania.

"Man," Qwerty whispered to his friend, "I've never seen so many dead white guys in one place at one time."

"Quiet!" Joey scolded him. "This is, like, historic!"

"Which one is George Washington?" Qwerty asked.

"He's not here. He's with the Continental Army in New York."

"How do you *know* that?" marveled Qwerty.

"The History Channel, doofus."

Franklin shot the boys a look and put his finger to his lips to tell them to keep quiet.

Qwerty and Joey looked around. What was most surprising about the men in this room was their age. Even Joey, who certainly knew his history, assumed that the Founding Fathers were a bunch of old men. But the men in this room appeared to be much younger than Joey expected. In fact, John Hancock was thirty-nine. John Adams was forty-two. Benjamin Rush was thirty-two. Thomas Jefferson was thirty-three. At seventy years old, Benjamin Franklin was, by far, the oldest man in the room.

Nevertheless, these young men looked *tired.* Jefferson had arrived in Philadelphia on May 14 after the long trip from Virginia. He had started writing the Declaration of Independence on June 13 and turned in what he considered to be a finished draft on June 28. Since that day, the other delegates had been arguing over it, picking it apart line by line, suggesting changes and arguing some more.

Everyone was worn out, especially Thomas Jefferson. He didn't like it when they fiddled with his words.

Some of the changes they made were minor. The phrase "neglected utterly" was changed to "utterly neglected." "A people who mean to be free" was changed to "a free people." The words "unremitting injuries" was changed to "repeated injuries." With each little change, though, Jefferson grew more irritated.

Other changes were big ones. In Jefferson's original draft, he included a paragraph condemning slavery, which he wrote was "an assemblage of horrors." Despite the fact that he himself owned slaves, Jefferson hoped the practice of slavery would be abolished once America declared its independence. After all, he wrote right there in the third line that "all men are created equal."

But the delegates from South Carolina and Georgia strongly opposed the paragraph about slavery. Slaves were used to pick cotton and work the tobacco fields in those colonies. If an antislavery paragraph was included in the Declaration, the southern states would surely refuse to be a part of the new nation.

A Declaration by the Representatives of the UNITED STATES
OF AMERICA, in General Congress assembled.

When in the course of human events it becomes necessary for one people to
dissolve the political bands which have connected them with another, and to
-sume among the powers of the earth the separate and equal station to
which the laws of nature & of nature's god entitle them, a decent respect
to the opinions of mankind requires that they should declare the causes
which impel them to the separation.

We hold these truths to be self-evident; that all men are
created equal, that they are endowed by their creator with
inherent & inalienable rights; that among these are the
life, & liberty, & the pursuit of happiness; that to secure these rights, go-
-vernments are instituted among men, deriving their just powers from
the consent of the governed; that whenever any form of government
becomes destructive of these ends, it is the right of the people to alter
or to abolish it, & to institute new government, laying it's foundation on
such principles & organising it's powers in such form, as to them shall
seem most likely to effect their safety & happiness. prudence indeed
will dictate that governments long established should not be changed for
light & transient causes: and accordingly all experience hath shewn that
mankind are more disposed to suffer while evils are sufferable, than to
right themselves by abolishing the forms to which they are accustomed. but
when a long train of abuses & usurpations [begun at a distinguished period,
&] pursuing invariably the same object, evinces a design to reduce
them under absolute Despotism, it is their right, it is their duty, to throw off such
+ & to provide new guards for their future security. such has
been the patient sufferance of these colonies; & such is now the necessity
which constrains them to expunge their former systems of government.
the history of the present king of Great Britain is a history of unremitting injuries and
usurpations, [among which appears no solitary fact repeated to contra-
dict the uniform tenor of the rest, all of which have in direct object the

After a heated discussion, the paragraph about slavery was deleted. The delegates decided that a nation that disagreed on this particular issue was better than no nation at all. First, declare independence, they agreed. Slavery could be addressed at a later date.

After a week of watching his Declaration ripped apart and insulted, Thomas Jefferson had good reason to be in a bad mood. In later years he would say the changes to his text had been "mutilations."

"Are they gonna sign it now?" Qwerty whispered to Joey.

"I don't know."

After all the work they had put into the Declaration, some of the delegates were still not sure that declaring independence from England was the right thing to do. The New York delegation in particular was divided. Several of their delegates were ready to form a new nation. Others were still opposed to the idea.

"How much more convincing do you require?" thundered John Adams at the reluctant New Yorkers. "First King George taxed our sugar! Then he refused to allow us to issue money! The Stamp Act taxed anything printed on paper. Then we were forcibly required to house and feed British soldiers in our homes! And finally, our king declares that England has the right to make laws for the colonies. That is quite enough for me. I say, America must be free!"

Murmurs of "here here!" and muted conversations rumbled through the room.

"Fifty British warships arrived at Sandy Hook, New Jersey, on the twenty-ninth of June," John Hancock informed the delegates. "On July the first, fifty-three more docked outside Charleston, South Carolina. Just yesterday we received information that the British have landed on Staten Island in New York. We have but little time, gentlemen!"

More buzzing discussions swirled around the room.

Slowly, Benjamin Franklin rose from his seat and struggled to his feet, using his cane for support. A hush fell over the room in respect for the old man.

"I have lived many years," he announced. "I am twice the age of some of you. Perhaps the only benefit of age is a certain degree of wisdom. If I have learned one thing in my life it is this: Make haste . . . slowly."

Thomas Jefferson stood up.

"Will Dr. Franklin be so good as to peruse this document," he said, "and suggest such alterations as his more enlarged view of the subject will dictate?"

"I would be most honored."

Each of the other delegates already had a copy of the Declaration on the table in front of him. Some had scribbled comments in the margins using the quill pens that sat on each table. A fresh copy was given to Franklin, and he began to read it out loud.

"When, in the Course of human events, it becomes necessary for one people to dissolve the political bands which have connected them with another, and to assume, among the powers of the earth, the separate and equal station to which the Laws of Nature and of Nature's God entitle them, a decent respect to the opinions of mankind requires that they should declare the causes which impel them to the separation . . ."

Franklin paused for a moment to absorb those words, which basically stated that the Declaration would explain why the colonies had decided to break away from England. Then he continued.

"We hold these truths to be sacred and undeniable: That all men are created equal; that they are endowed by their Creator with certain unalienable Rights; that among these are Life, Liberty, and the pursuit of Happiness; That, to secure these rights, Governments are instituted among Men, deriving their just powers from the consent of the governed . . ."

Franklin nodded his head. Jefferson certainly had a way with words. In such simple and beautiful language, he had communicated that in America the people would control the government and not the other way around. No person would be better than any other.

". . . that whenever any Form of Government becomes destructive of these ends, it is the Right of the People to alter or to abolish it . . ."

Franklin nodded again. Of course. If a government is unjust, the people should have the right to get rid of it and replace it with a better one.

He continued to read, ticking off Jefferson's list of twenty-seven complaints the American colonists had against King George III and the

British government. Many of these concerned unfair taxes and the presence of British troops in America. After each complaint, Franklin nodded his head again.

"We, therefore, the Representatives of the United States of America—"

Franklin stopped for a moment and looked up. The words *The United States of America* had never appeared in print before.

"That is most pleasing to the ear," he said. He read the next few lines silently before concluding . . .

" . . . That these United Colonies are, and of Right ought to be FREE AND INDEPENDENT STATES; that they are absolved from all Allegiance to the British Crown, and that all political Connection between them and the State of Great Britain, is, and ought to be, totally dissolved; and that, as Free and Independent States, they have full Power to levy War, conclude Peace, contract Alliances, establish Commerce, and do all other Acts and Things which Independent States may of right do. And for the support of this declaration, with a firm Reliance on the Protection of divine Providence, we

mutually pledge to each other our lives, our Fortunes, and our sacred Honor."

All was quiet in the large room.

Joey Dvorak wondered if people who live through and witness historic events like this one realize at the moment that they are experiencing something incredibly important that will be remembered for centuries. Or, does it seem like any other moment in their lives? Joey, for one, had goose bumps on his arms.

Everyone was looking at Franklin, the elder statesman, to gauge his opinion of the document.

"It is good," he reported. "It is very good."

Thomas Jefferson let out a sigh of relief.

"I have but one small suggestion," Franklin added.

Jefferson grimaced, clenching his fist.

"My suggestion is self-evident," Franklin said, holding up a hand to calm his younger colleague.

"It is not self-evident to *me*," snarled Jefferson.

"Nor me," snapped Adams.

"What *is* it, Dr. Franklin?" John Hancock asked.

"You wrote 'We hold these Truths to be sacred and undeniable that all men are created equal,'"

Franklin told Jefferson. "I believe 'self-evident' would be more concise, more forceful."

After a brief discussion, the delegates agreed, and the sentence was changed to read, *We hold these Truths to be self-evident: That all men are created equal* . . . It was Benjamin Franklin's one contribution to the Declaration of Independence.

"It is finished then," John Hancock announced.

After a rousing chorus of "here here!" and "huzzah!" all those assembled agreed that together they had created a document that not only served the purpose of declaring independence from England, but also suggested a new and innovative form of government. Although it wasn't perfect, they had created one of the most important and treasured documents in world history.

And that was precisely why Ashley Quadrel was standing outside the statehouse at that very moment, his revolver tucked inside the waistband of his pants.

13

Sticking With the Plan

"This *is* Independence Hall!" Ashley Quadrel barked at Sally Franklin as they approached the instantly recognizable building.

"It is the statehouse," Sally insisted disgustedly. She was sick of leading this foolish and oddly dressed man through the streets of Philadelphia. People had been staring. She didn't appreciate being called stupid. If he hadn't had that silly-looking gun, she thought, she would have given him a piece of her mind.

When Sally saw the guard stationed outside the statehouse door with a rifle in his hands, she was relieved. Her father was safe. This lunatic was not going to be able to storm into the statehouse and shoot him, if that was what he had been planning.

Ashley Quadrel saw the guard too. It hadn't occurred to him beforehand that anyone would be guarding Independence Hall. He'd figured he would be able to walk right in and surprise them all.

But this guy had a gun. It was probably loaded, and the guard probably knew how to use it. He looked mean, too.

Quadrel scrambled to think of ways he could get into Independence Hall. He could attempt to overpower the guard. But there was a good chance the guard would overpower *him*, and possibly kill him.

He could take Sally Franklin with him and threaten to shoot her if anyone tried to stop him. But taking hostages was unpredictable. So many things could go wrong. Quadrel had seen enough cops-and-robbers movies to know that hostage takers always got shot or at least caught in the end.

Sally Franklin looked around nervously. She could make a run for it and get away from this crazy man. She knew it, and he knew it.

Quadrel looked Independence Hall up and

down carefully. That's when he figured another way to get inside the building.

"It's time for you to split," he instructed Sally.

"I beg your pardon?"

"Scram," Quadrel ordered.

"Huh?"

"Beat it!" Quadrel shouted.

Sally didn't know what *split*, *scram*, or *beat it* meant. But she gathered from Quadrel's hand gestures and tone of voice that her services were no longer required. She dashed off before he had the chance to change his mind.

Carefully, like he was taking a stroll in the park, Ashley Quadrel walked around the back of Independence Hall. No guard was stationed there. A wooden scaffolding—the kind that might be used for making public announcements—was attached to the rear of the building. Quadrel hopped up onto a plank.

From that plank, he was able to reach a windowsill a few feet up with his toe. Carefully, he climbed onto the windowsill.

The window was locked. Quadrel searched for something he could grab on to and found a row of bricks that jutted out a few inches from the wall. As he hoisted himself up, he thought how fortunate it was that colonial buildings had such fancy architecture. If he ever tried to climb a *modern* statehouse, he would never get past the first floor. They were all steel, concrete, and windows that didn't even have sills.

Quadrel climbed higher, digging a toe into a crevice here, grabbing with his hand onto a window ledge there. For a heavy man, he was nimble. Fully aware that anyone in the stone courtyard behind the statehouse could knock him off the wall with a bullet or even a rock, Quadrel climbed as quickly as possible.

Finally, he reached the top of the building, which came almost to a point. He had noticed from the street level that there was an opening up there, and that it looked large enough for a man to squeeze into. Quadrel slung one leg into that opening, and then the other leg. He was sitting at the edge there, the bottom of his body in the building and the top half out of it.

He could feel something below his feet—a thick piece of wood, maybe. It felt solid, so Quadrel put his weight on it and lowered himself until his entire body was inside the building. He was crouching on the wooden beam, balancing himself by putting a hand against the posts on either side of him.

When he felt steady enough to look down, Quadrel was surprised to see that hanging directly below the wooden beam was a large, circular object about four feet across. He sat down. Upon closer examination he could make out the words, PROCLAIM LIBERTY THROUGHOUT ALL THE LAND TO ALL THE INHABITANTS THEREOF.

A smile broke out across Ashley Quadrel's face as he realized what he was sitting on.

The Liberty Bell.

The Liberty Bell! Of course! The bell tower was at the top of Independence Hall! They would ring the bell after they had voted for independence. Next to the Statue of Liberty, the Liberty Bell was probably the most famous symbol of America.

And I'm sitting on it!

It was a massive thing. Made from a mixture of copper and tin, the bell was twelve feet around the lip and 2,080 pounds. It had been made in England, but hung in the Pennsylvania statehouse in 1753.

Quadrel slid down the side of the bell, landing gingerly on a plank below it. Looking up at the inside of the bell, he smiled. The famous crack in the Liberty Bell wasn't there yet. That would happen seventy years later, on Washington's birthday.

As was his nature, Ashley Quadrel paused for a moment to consider what havoc he could bring about in this particular situation.

Stealing the Liberty Bell! Now *that* would get him some attention. The bell would look great in his living room, too.

Nah, Quadrel reasoned. How would he ever get the thing *out* of there? He would need a truck and some really big guys and—

Wait a minute! Rather than steal the Liberty Bell, he could just cut it loose! It was only being held on to the wooden beam by rope. If he cut the rope, the bell would go crashing down through several stories and land on the first floor, where the Founding Fathers were about to sign the Declaration of Independence!

What a hoot it would be to have all those men with their powdered wigs running for their lives! What delicious irony it would be if he was able to use the Liberty Bell *itself* to crush American liberty forever!

Ashley Quadrel, in case you haven't gathered by now, was a dangerously disturbed individual.

Quadrel shook his head. No. As tempting as it was to drop the Liberty Bell on top of the Founding Fathers and pull off the most spectacular practical joke in history, he had a job to do. He had come to kidnap George Washington, change the Declaration of Independence into a Declaration of Loyalty, and take it home with him. That was the plan, and he was determined to stick with it.

Being careful not to step on any creaky boards, Ashley Quadrel tiptoed down several flights of narrow stairs until he was standing alone in the large second-floor hallway of Independence Hall.

He was directly above the room where the Founding Fathers were about to declare America's independence.

"Gentlemen," John Hancock announced, rising from his chair, "the time has come to cast our vote for or against this Declaration we have created, for or against independence from Great Britain. Will the delegation from Massachusetts please honor us by casting the first vote?"

"Aye!" the Massachusetts delegates spoke as one.

"The delegation from Virginia . . ." said Hancock.

"Aye!"

"New Jersey?"

"Aye!"

One by one, the representatives from each of the thirteen colonies cast a vote. With the exception of New York, every colony voted in favor of independence. The New York delegates were still undecided on the issue.

With the vote completed, silence hung in the air for a few seconds. John Hancock pounded his gavel on the table once. "The ayes have it," he announced. "This Declaration of Independence is hereby approved."

"Here here!"

"Huzzah!"

It was like a giant exhale filled the room. These men had been anticipating this moment for weeks, months—and some of them for years. Now it had finally happened. Smiles broke out on many faces. Tears slid down many cheeks. John Hancock banged his gavel again to call the room to order. "Gentlemen," he said as he reached for his quill, "we must afix our signatures to this parchment."

"Not so fast!" shouted Ashley Quadrel as he burst into the room, eyes on fire and waving his gun around wildly.

14

Hero of the British Empire

Ashley Quadrel was so excited that he almost tripped over his own feet as he barged into the main hall of the statehouse. He could hardly believe he had pulled it off. There they were—the Founding Fathers of the United States of America—all in one room. He had them right where he wanted them. It was almost *too* easy.

"Don't write your John Hancock down just yet!" he instructed John Hancock.

"Who is this man?" Hancock demanded. "And how does he know my name?"

"I am Ashley Quadrel!" Quadrel announced. "I am your future king!"

Qwerty and Joey were so stunned, it took them a moment to realize what was happening. Quadrel took advantage of the confusion in the room to cross over to the front door and lock it so the guard could not come in the building.

"He's crazy!" Qwerty finally stood up and shouted.

Quadrel wheeled around to see where the voice had come from.

"Well, if it isn't my little friend from back home in New Jersey," he sneered at the boy. "We meet again."

"You'll never get away with this!" shouted Joey, who had seen countless movies in which that line had been shouted and always wanted to use it himself.

"Get away with *what?*" Quadrel asked innocently.

"Get away with whatever it is you're planning on getting away with!" Qwerty yelled.

"We'll see about that!" Quadrel smirked.

"Why are Franklin's servants acquainted with this intruder?" John Adams asked.

"None of your business!" shouted Quadrel. "Everyone freeze!"

Having never seen a police show on television—much less a television at *all*—the delegates stared at Quadrel with confused expressions on their faces.

"That means don't move or he'll shoot," translated Joey.

"Is that a pistol?" asked Thomas Jefferson.

"Of *course* it's a pistol!" Quadrel replied indignantly. "Haven't you people ever seen a revolver before?"

"No," fifty-six voices replied.

"It holds six bullets," Qwerty informed them. "Every time you pull the trigger, this round thing turns a little and the next bullet moves into position to fire."

"Ingenious!" proclaimed Franklin, who despite being a nonviolent man, could always appreciate a clever invention.

"Are you a loyalist?" John Hancock asked Quadrel.

"That's right," Quadrel said, "I'm a loyalist. Your revolution is over right now, gentlemen. I came here to make America British forever. I'll be the hero of the British Empire!"

"He's a madman!" declared John Adams.

"Maybe I am," Quadrel said with his evil, cackling laugh, "but you boys had better do as I say if you want to see the Fifth of July."

"What is it you desire?" Jefferson asked.

Quadrel scanned the room carefully. "Which one of you is George Washington?" he asked, not seeing the familiar face.

"General Washington is in New York with the Continental Army," John Adams said. Joey nudged Qwerty, mouthing the words "I *told* you."

"Don't lie to me!" screamed Quadrel. "He's hiding, isn't he? Where? Tell me or I'll kill you all!"

"He's not lying," Joey said. "Washington isn't here."

Ashley Quadrel didn't like surprises. George Washington was "the Father of Our Country," wasn't he? And this was a meeting of the Founding Fathers of the country, wasn't it? So why wasn't Washington here? How could they have a meeting of the Founding Fathers without the chief father?

Even in his warped mind, Quadrel realized they couldn't just call up George Washington on the phone and get him on the next train to Philadelphia. There were no telephones *or* locomotives in 1776. Quadrel's brilliant plan was collapsing around him. Sweat began to bead up on his forehead.

"Okay," Quadrel said desperately. "Forget about George Washington. I don't need him, anyway. Here is my demand. You, Mr. Jefferson! I want you to rewrite the Declaration of Independence. You will turn it into a Declaration of Loyalty to the king of England. And then you will give it to me. That's what I *really* want."

Thomas Jefferson stared daggers at Ashley Quadrel. First his colleagues had revised his Declaration until it was almost unrecognizable. Now this lunatic was going to change it into a Declaration of Loyalty. Jefferson was beginning to wish he had stayed home in Virginia.

All eyes turned to John Hancock, who held the Declaration of Independence. He couldn't decide whether to hand over the parchment or risk getting shot to defend it.

"If we are willing to confront the greatest military power on the earth, we must be willing to confront a single man!" declared John Adams. "Charge him! He cannot shoot us all!"

"Oh yeah?" Quadrel sneered, waving his gun around. "Which one of you wants to die first?

How about you, Mr. Adams? Or Mr. Jefferson here. I could shoot the two of you right now and neither of you will ever be president!"

Adams and Jefferson looked at Quadrel, confused. Neither man even knew what a president *was*, much less that they would one day have such a job. Thomas Jefferson seriously considered jumping on the funny-looking little man and trying to wrestle him to the ground.

For a long, tortured minute, nobody moved or spoke. John Hancock still gripped the Declaration. Somebody would have to give in.

Benjamin Franklin, frail and feeble, finally rose to his feet. "I am old and good for nothing," Franklin said.

"Don't, Mr. Franklin!" Qwerty shouted.

But Franklin held up a hand to quiet the boy. Slowly, he walked over to Hancock's table, leaning heavily on his cane. He held out his hand, and Hancock gave Franklin the Declaration. "You win, Mr. Quadrel," Franklin said gravely. "Let none of us resort to violence."

"Well, that's more like it," Quadrel said, relieved. He knew that if one of the Founding Fathers had actually put up a fight, he would be finished.

"Dr. Franklin!" exclaimed the alarmed John Hancock. "Do you know what you are doing?"

"There is a time to fight," Franklin said sadly, "and a time to flee. Mr. Quadrel, I am afraid, has the upper hand in this disagreement."

"Now you're talking sense," Quadrel agreed.

Franklin rolled the Declaration up like a scroll, slowly walked over to Thomas Jefferson, and handed him the parchment. "Do as he says," Franklin said, sighing.

"Don't do it!" Qwerty screamed.

"Mr. Quadrel," Franklin said, hushing the boy with a finger to his lips, "or shall I refer to you as Your Majesty?"

"Quadrel is fine," Ashley replied.

"We are all civilized gentlemen, Mr. Quadrel," Franklin said. "In a civilized society it is customary for a defeated nation to share a glass of wine with its opponent. Anything less would be barbaric. Will you join me upstairs to toast your victory while Mr. Jefferson rewrites the Declaration to your specifications?"

Quadrel looked Franklin over carefully. Was the old man trying to pull something? But Franklin's face was as innocent as a baby's, and in the end Quadrel couldn't resist being honored by one of the most famous men in the world. "Well, okay," he agreed, "but I'm warning you, don't try any funny stuff."

"Servants!" Franklin called, prompting Qwerty and Joey to dash over. "Carry me to the second-floor meeting room, will you please? And someone please fetch a bottle of Pennsylvania's finest Madiera. Nothing but the best for Mr. Quadrel."

Ashley Quadrel puffed up his chest with pride. For the first time in his adult life, he was being treated with the respect he felt he deserved. The Founding Fathers of the United States of America were sitting there in fear of him. They were going to rewrite the Declaration of Independence . . . because *he* had told them to! Life was sweet.

Quadrel thought about all those kids back in elementary school who had teased him for being stupid. All those coaches who had said he couldn't play ball. All those girls who didn't want to go out with him. All those rock bands that told him to get lost. All those companies that rejected his brilliant inventions. All those psychologists who tried to figure out why he behaved the way he did.

If only they could see me *now*, Quadrel thought as he climbed the stairs to the second floor alongside Benjamin Franklin. They would know he had finally achieved greatness. They would regret underestimating his potential. He sure showed *them!*

Franklin had the boys carry him into one of the several rooms that were on the second floor of the statehouse. The whale-oil lanterns on the walls had not been lit, and with the curtains drawn the room was somewhat dark. There wasn't much to look at, anyway. A long table with eight chairs around it. Portraits of old white men on the walls wearing powdered wigs. A fancy chandelier.

Franklin took a seat at the table and gestured for Quadrel to sit down opposite him. Quadrel rested the heavy gun on the table, but did not let it slip from his hand. Qwerty and Joey stood awkwardly behind Franklin, desperately trying to think of ways to get at that gun.

A young man wearing a plain white shirt and breeches came into the room with a bottle and two glasses. Franklin poured the wine and dismissed the man who had delivered it.

"I would like to propose a toast to the future king of America, Mr. Ashley Quadrel," he said as he raised his glass. "May you be at war with your vices, at peace with your neighbors, and let every New Year find you a better man."

"I'll drink to that," Quadrel said, and he took a long gulp from the glass.

Qwerty and Joey were sure the wine was poisoned. They were positive that Quadrel's eyes would roll up and he'd fall off the chair in a heap on the floor, unconscious. Why else would Franklin just cave in to Quadrel's demands without putting up any resistance?

But Quadrel's eyes did not roll up and he didn't topple over. The wine had not been poisoned.

"Ahhhh," Quadrel said, savoring the taste.

Off in the corner of the room, almost in the shadows, was a machine of some sort. It was mounted on a wooden stand about six feet high, and had a glass ball about the size of a basketball in the middle. There was a crank on the right side that was attached to the glass ball with a pulley system. Next to the machine, on the floor, was a wooden box with forty glass jars in it.

Quadrel's eyes, having adapted to the dark room, noticed the device. A frustrated inventor himself, he often noticed unusual machines. "What's that contraption?" he asked Franklin.

"Oh that?" Franklin replied. "I call that the Armonica. It is one of my more recent inventions."

Ashley Quadrel knew about Franklin's lightning rod, his stove, and his bifocal eye glasses. All were world famous inventions. But he had never heard of the Armonica. His interest was piqued. The Armonica might be something worth stealing.

"Some kind of a musical instrument, is it?" he asked, getting up from his seat to have a closer look.

"Very perceptive, Mr. Quadrel," Franklin replied. "With the aid of a flywheel, the crank puts into motion the glass hemisphere, which is mounted on an iron spindle. When one places a moistened finger to the glass, it produces tones that are remarkably sweet in nature. Even an individual with no musical ability can sound as practiced as a virtuoso."

Quadrel liked the sound of that. He had wanted to play a musical instrument since the age of five, but had not been successful with the guitar, piano, saxophone, or drums. He approached the machine, tucking the gun into the waistband of his pants to free up his hands. Franklin remained in his seat.

Turning the crank slowly, Quadrel watched as a belt going from the crank to the spindle made the glass ball rotate. When he reversed direction of the crank, the ball turned in the opposite direction. He licked a finger and held it against the ball. No sounds were produced.

"The glass hemisphere must be spun more rapidly," Franklin called from his seat.

Quadrel turned the crank faster and licked his finger a second time. Still no sound was produced when he touched the glass ball. "The thing is busted," Quadrel complained.

"More rapidly," advised Franklin.

Quadrel turned the crank as fast as he could. The glass ball was spinning at several hundred revolutions per second now. Quadrel moistened his finger a third time, and brought it up to the spinning ball.

Bzzzzzzzzzzzzzzzzzzzzzzzzzzzzzzzzzzztttttttttt!

A flash of white light jumped from the ball, across the quarter-inch gap, and over to the nearest object—Ashley Quadrel's finger. The walls echoed with a *craaaaaaccckk* that could be heard throughout the building. A jolt of electricity ripped through Quadrel's body almost instantly as he collapsed. The gun clattered to the wood floor. The smell of sulfur wafted across the room.

Ashley Quadrel was not moving.

15

Hanging Together

Qwerty and Joey stood there, too stunned to move. Ashley Quadrel was lying on his back, eyes closed, mouth wide open.

"Little strokes fell great oaks," Franklin said to break the silence.

"Is he . . . dead?" Joey asked.

"No," Franklin said with a chuckle. "He has merely received a healthy electric shock. In a half hour or so he should regain his senses. His arms and neck may be numb for the remainder of the evening."

Qwerty grabbed the gun and gave it to Franklin, who examined it carefully. "Ingenious!" he declared.

"So you made up all that stuff about the Armonica?" Joey asked. "It doesn't even exist, does it?"

"Certainly it exists," Franklin replied. "But this machine is not the Armonica."

"Then what is it?" Qwerty asked.

"I call it an electrical *battery*," Franklin replied. He said the word battery as if the boys had never heard of such a thing. "It is quite simple, actually, but rather effective. A full charge is sufficient to kill a chicken."

"You killed a chicken with that thing?" asked Qwerty.

"The meat is most uncommonly tender, I assure you."

Franklin struggled to his feet. Each of the boys took one of his elbows and helped him down the staircase.

"That guy Quadrel is crazy," Qwerty said.

"People such as myself, who live a long life and drink to the bottom of the cup, must expect to meet some of the dregs," Franklin commented.

"The important thing is," Joey said, "he didn't have the chance to mess with the Declaration."

"I have been a printer all my life," Franklin told

them. "The Declaration of Independence is merely ink on parchment. Its ideas cannot be destroyed or stolen. Our cause is the cause of all mankind."

In the main meeting room, the delegates from the thirteen colonies still sat. When they saw Franklin coming down the stairs, they stopped their conversations and looked up expectantly. Thomas Jefferson held the Declaration tightly in his hand. He had not altered a word of it.

"My deepest apologies for the interruption, gentlemen," Franklin told the group.

"What was that infernal sound?" John Hancock asked. "And where is that loon?"

"Mr. Quadrel accidentally absorbed a small electrical charge," Franklin replied with a smirk. "He is . . . taking a nap. Snug as a bug in a rug. It may be wise to secure his wrists in the eventuality of an early awakening. Pennsylvania's finest rope, please. Nothing but the best for Mr. Quadrel!"

"Here, here!" some delegates chanted, while others guffawed enthusiastically.

"Leave it to Franklin!" John Adams chortled.

"Once again the great Dr. Franklin has proven the usefulness of electric fire," Jefferson added.

"No gains without pains," Franklin said, chuckling.

"Hip hip hooray!"

"Hip hip hooray!"

"Hip hip hooray!"

When order had been restored, Jefferson handed the Declaration to John Hancock, who steered the meeting back to the business the delegates had been engaged in before Ashley Quadrel had interrupted things. Taking his quill in hand, Hancock leaned over the parchment and wrote his name below the bottom line in big, bold, flowing letters.

"King George must be able to read it without the necessity of putting on his spectacles," he said.

The other delegates stood up and formed a line at Hancock's desk. One by one, they signed the paper. Some of them took a deep breath or said a silent prayer before committing what was—in effect—treason against their own country.

"There must be no pulling in different ways," Hancock told the group. "We must all hang together."

"Yes," Franklin agreed, "we must indeed all hang together, or we shall most assuredly hang separately."

"That's pretty funny!" Qwerty whispered to Joey.

"It's also true," his friend whispered back.

When the last man had signed, Hancock called the meeting to order again and asked the delegates to return to their seats. The work was not done. In fact, it was just beginning. Hancock assigned each delegate a different responsibility.

First, a printer had to be hired to print copies of the Declaration of Independence. Copies had to be sent out to all assemblies, conventions, committees, and councils of safety. The Declaration was to be proclaimed in each of the thirteen colonies—now independent states. It had to be read aloud at public gatherings, posted on bulletin boards, and printed in newspapers.

Once word crossed the Atlantic that independence had been declared, war with England would most certainly follow. The commanding officers of the Continental Army needed to receive copies of the Declaration. It had to be distributed among the soldiers and read to the ones who were not literate.

Ammunition and other military supplies had to be manufactured, gathered, or purchased. A new and improved musket had to be designed. A ring of logs had to be floated across the Delaware and other rivers at American port cities to slow down

British warships. Alliances had to be established with foreign countries that could be helpful to the American cause.

"The way to secure peace is to be prepared for war," Franklin informed Qwerty and Joey.

Medical supplies had to be distributed. Money had to be printed. A national post office had to be established. Hundreds of other details had to be attended to before the thirteen colonies could successfully fight a war and eventually form a government.

"We have an important assignment for you," Hancock told Franklin.

"I am too old to be a soldier," Franklin said.

"We want you to be our ambassador to France."

"I accept," replied Franklin. "While a soldier must be willing to die for his country, a diplomat need only lie for his country."

"This meeting is adjourned," Hancock said, pounding his gavel. Delegates streamed from the room to carry out their responsibilities.

"Nothing is left now but to fight it out," Franklin said, sighing.

"What can we do to help?" Joey asked.

"Would you like to ring the bell?" said Franklin.

"What bell?" Qwerty replied.

"The Liberty Bell, doofus!" Joey told him.

The boys ran upstairs two steps at a time, racing to beat the other one for the chance to ring the most famous bell in history. Gasping for breath, they reached the bell tower at nearly the same time.

Pausing for just a moment to marvel at their good luck, they reached over to grab a thick rope that hung down from the bell's clapper. When they yanked it, the clapper slammed into the side of the bell and produced an earsplitting *bonnnnnnnngggggg*. The boys covered their ears to muffle the sound. It was painful, but they couldn't resist ringing the bell again. And again. And again. Soon, church bells all over Philadelphia were ringing, too.

Gleefully, the boys dashed back downstairs. The big meeting room was empty now. Some of the delegates were standing around chatting with one another in front of the statehouse. A crowd was starting to gather. People were curious about why the statehouse bell had chimed. Benjamin Franklin was engaged in a conversation with a man from the militia.

"I guess we'd better go now," Joey suggested to Qwerty.

"Yeah, I guess."

"So . . . how do we do it?"

At that moment Qwerty realized—for the first time—that he had forgotten to make arrangements to bring them back to the twenty-first century.

16

Independence Day

It was five o'clock in New Jersey.

Mr. and Mrs. Stevens were at their respective offices, finishing up their work for the day.

Madison Stevens was playing with toys at the after-school program she attended. Her teacher had already told the kids several times to start cleaning up.

Barbara Stevens was finishing a rehearsal for *Bye Bye Birdie*, which the high school would be putting on in two weeks. Every day she picked up Madison and they came home together.

Miss Vera Vaughn was walking out of Thomas Edison Middle School. During the long staff meeting after school, she had been thinking and worrying about Qwerty Stevens. Where had he gone after he left school? Who was the strange man who had answered the phone at his house? Miss Vaughn was about to get into her car and drive home, but she decided to walk over to Qwerty's house again and see if anyone was around.

The Stevens house was empty. It had been empty since early afternoon, when Ashley Quadrel had shimmied up the drainpipe and used the Anytime Anywhere Machine to send himself to Philadelphia. A never-ending army of toasters flew across the computer screen in Qwerty's bedroom. The Anytime Anywhere Machine was still on, but there was nobody at the computer to hit the ESCAPE key.

In Philadelphia, Joey Dvorak was out-of-his-mind furious.

"You . . . forgot?!" he screamed at Qwerty. "How could you forget something like that?"

"I just . . . forgot to remember," Qwerty moaned, hanging his head in shame.

What Qwerty forgot to remember was to arrange for somebody to sit at his computer and bring them back at the end of their trip. The first time he had used the Anytime Anywhere Machine, his sister Barbara had brought him home safely.

Qwerty realized that he had *also* forgotten about his doctor appointment that afternoon. But in light of the situation, a doctor appointment didn't seem all that important.

"Now we're stuck here!" Joey yelled. "We're stuck here *forever!*"

"Barb will go into my room and figure out what's happening," Qwerty said, trying his best to be optimistic. "She'll bring us home."

"What if your mom turns off the computer?" Joey asked. "Or what if there's a blackout or power surge or something?"

"Then we're in trouble," admitted Qwerty.

"My dad's gonna kill me," moaned Joey. "He's gonna freakin' kill me."

"He won't be able to," Qwerty said glumly. "If we're stuck here, your dad is never gonna see you again."

With that, the boys began to sob uncontrollably.

In West Orange, Barbara and Madison Stevens

got home before their parents. Barbara preheated the oven and took a chicken casserole out of the refrigerator. Madison began to set the table for dinner.

"Where's Qwerty?" she asked her older sister.

"He had a doctor appointment after school," Barbara replied. "He should be home any minute."

"Oooh, can I play on the computer?" Madison asked her sister. In school, the kids had just started learning how to use computers. Madison had borrowed a "Make-Up Mandy" program from one of the girls in her class, and she was anxious to try it out. Qwerty always hogged the computer when he was home, and he didn't like her touching it.

"Okay," Barbara agreed.

Madison grabbed "Make-Up Mandy" and ran upstairs into Qwerty's room. When she touched the mouse, the screen saver left the screen. Madison expected to see a gray "desktop," but instead there was a virtual tour of Philadelphia and photos of Qwerty, Joey, and Ashley Quadrel. "Barbara!" she called. "I need help!"

"I'm cooking dinner," Barb called from downstairs. "What's the matter?"

"I don't know how to load 'Make-Up Mandy.'"

"Try to figure it out on your own," Barbara yelled.

Mr. and Mrs. Stevens were in their cars, driving home from work.

Miss Vaughn was on foot, heading for the Stevens house.

In Philadelphia, Qwerty and Joey were sitting on the curb in front of the statehouse, crying their eyes out.

"We'll never see our parents again," sniffled Qwerty.

"Who's gonna take care of us?"

"Nobody," Qwerty replied, trying to get a grip on himself. "We'll have to take care of ourselves."

"Kids probably did that all the time in colonial days," said Joey. "I mean, the average person only lived to be about fifty. Lots of kids must have grown up with no parents."

"We won't have to go to school," Qwerty noted, brightening. Suddenly, being stuck in 1776 appeared to have certain advantages. "We could get jobs. I could fix machines or something. And you could—"

The Pennsylvania militia marched up the street. The news of independence must have gotten out, because there was a new sense of purpose to the soldiers. They marched more crisply. The drummer boy banged the skins a little more sharply. There was the unmistakable look of determination on the faces of the militiamen.

Joey Dvorak stood up and wiped the tears from his face with his sleeve. "I'm gonna join up!" he announced. "I can handle a weapon. I can play the drums. I'm gonna stay right here and fight for my country."

"You're gonna get yourself killed, dude," Qwerty warned.

"Maybe I will," Joey said. "But what better cause is there to die for? I mean, look where we are! The American Revolution is about to begin! I could be part of it! Part of history. How cool would that be?"

"It's not some game," Qwerty argued. "You can't just hit the reset button and start over again if somebody shoots you."

"Qwerty," Joey said to his friend, "what do I have to lose?"

Qwerty looked at Joey and saw that he was right. They would never be going back to West Orange. They no longer had families, friends, or homes. They had no money, no possessions. They didn't even own the clothes on their backs.

"Well," Qwerty said, "if you're gonna join up, then I'm gonna join up with you. We're all we have. We gotta stick together."

They went over to Benjamin Franklin, who looked like he was on his way back home.

"Mr. Franklin!" Joey said urgently. "We have decided that we want to join the Continental Army."

Franklin looked at the boys, puzzled.

"If we're not old enough to fight," Joey continued, "at least we could be drummer boys or play the bugle or something."

Franklin looked each boy in the eye. He could see they had been crying.

"And what is to become of your families?" he asked. "Your friends? Your . . . future?"

"We'd rather fight for independence," Qwerty said. He was too embarrassed to admit to Franklin that he had messed up and they were stuck in the eighteenth century . . . maybe forever.

"Independence is a most delicate thing," Franklin said, putting one arm around each of the boys. "When America was young, we needed our Mother England to protect us, to watch over us, to nurture us. Now our country is growing up and

ready to be independent. But you young men . . .
you are not yet ready for independence. You still
require your mothers."

"But—"

Franklin put a finger to his lips to hush the
boys. "Vessels large may venture more, but little
boats should keep near shore," he told the boys.
"Your time for independence will come . . . in a
few short years."

Qwerty and Joey burst into tears again.

In West Orange, Miss Vaughn was a block
away from the Stevens house. Mr. and Mrs.
Stevens were stuck in rush-hour traffic.

Madison Stevens was having trouble loading
"Make-Up Mandy." She had put the disk into the
drive, but nothing happened. She hit the
RETURN key repeatedly. "Barbara!" she called
downstairs.

"What?" Barbara was getting a little irritated.
She was trying to cook the casserole, make a salad,
pour drinks for everybody, and stir a rice side dish all
at the same time. She didn't have time to help
Madison with the computer. Their parents were due
home any minute. And where was Qwerty, anyway?

"There's stuff on the screen," Madison hollered.

"What kind of stuff?"

"Stuff about Philadelphia," Madison said, except that she was just learning how to read and said something that sounded like 'Pill-a-del-pee.' "And there's a picture of Qwerty and his friend and some other guy."

"Just turn off the computer and restart it," Barbara yelled.

Suddenly, Barbara stopped stirring her rice.

Philadelphia?

Qwerty and his friend and some other guy?

Barbara dropped her spoon in the pan and bolted out of the kitchen. "Stop!" she shrieked. "Ohmygod! Stop!"

As she pounded up the stairs, Barbara realized that Qwerty was not at his doctor appointment. He was in Philadelphia in the time of Benjamin Franklin. And if Madison turned off the computer, Qwerty and Joey would be staying there for a long, long time.

"Don't turn it off!" Barbara screamed as she ran into Qwerty's room.

One of the mysteries of the Information Age is why computers do not have obvious on/off switches. When you need to turn on a lamp, you usually know where to find the switch. When you want to turn on a TV, it's pretty easy to find the power button. But with computers it's not so easy. Some of them have an on/off switch in the back. Some of them don't have an on/off switch at all.

Madison, fortunately, could not find the on/off switch. She tried hitting the DELETE key. She tried hitting the SHIFT key. She tried hitting the OPTION key. She tried hitting the ENTER key. She even tried hitting the CAPS LOCK key.

And then she hit the ESCAPE key.

Out of nowhere, from a hundred miles and two centuries away, three bodies came hurtling into the room—Qwerty, Joey, and a very dazed and confused Ashley Quadrel, his wrists bound together in front of him with rope.

"Ooooff," Joey groaned as he hit the floor.

"Eeeeeeeeeeeeeeeeeeek!" screamed Madison.

"What the—" Quadrel muttered. "Where am I?"

Very quickly, Quadrel realized where he was, and he also realized that he'd better get out of there as quickly as possible. He got up, went to the window, raised it, and jumped out.

"Who was *that?*" Barbara asked, rushing over to look out the window.

"It's a long story," Qwerty replied, giving her a hug. He was just happy to be home.

17

A Deal

On the sidewalk outside the Stevens house, Miss Vera Vaughn was startled to see a man tumble out of a second-floor window. She watched, stunned and horrified, as Ashley Quadrel landed in the bushes in front of the house, bounced onto the front lawn, got up, and dashed down the street like he was running in a track meet.

Miss Vaughn hurried up the front steps and rang the bell. Madison came downstairs and opened the door. "May I help you?" she asked in her most polite voice.

"A man just fell out of the window upstairs!" Miss Vaughn exclaimed.

"No, he didn't," Madison replied calmly. "He *jumped* out the window upstairs."

"I saw him land in the bushes and run away!"

"He must be okay then," Madison reasoned.

Miss Vaughn rushed past Madison and went upstairs to Qwerty's bedroom, where she found Joey, Qwerty, and Barbara.

"Miss Vaughn!" Qwerty exclaimed. "What are *you* doing here?"

"I . . . was worried!" she replied. "You boys never came back to school, and when I called, a strange man answered the phone. So I decided to come over. And then this man, why, he just jumped out of the window!"

Qwerty and Joey burst out laughing.

"This is not funny!" Miss Vaughn said sharply. "You are in a heap of trouble, Qwerty. You completely plagiarized your report on the American Revolution. You'll probably fail the test on Thursday. You never came back to school all afternoon. Strangers have been answering your telephone. And now I find that people are jumping out the windows! I want to know what has been going on here!"

Qwerty sighed. He had hoped to keep the secret of the Anytime Anywhere Machine away from all grown-ups, but he had no choice.

He told her everything. He apologized for copying his report. He explained how he had found Thomas Edison's invention, how he had used it to go to Philadelphia on July 4, 1776, how Ashley Quadrel tried to sabotage the Declaration of Independence, and how Benjamin Franklin stopped him.

"And you expect me to believe that?" Miss Vaughn asked.

"I know it sounds a little crazy," Joey told her. "But it's true. I was there."

"I am going to have to talk to Dr. Pullman about the plagiarism," Miss Vaughn said, shaking her head. "I'm going to have to tell your parents, Qwerty."

Qwerty sank to his knees. "Please?" he begged. "Please don't tell anybody. I won't ever copy anything ever again. I promise."

"I'm sorry, Qwerty," Miss Vaughn replied. "Plagiarism is very serious. It's stealing."

"Can we make a deal?" Qwerty pleaded. "If I could *prove* to you that Joey and I went back to seventeen seventy-six, would you keep this plagiarism thing to yourself?"

"Qwerty, don't," Joey warned.

"You're going to prove it to me?" snorted Miss Vaughn. "Go ahead. *This* I'd like to see."

Qwerty sat Miss Vaughn down in his chair and snapped a picture of her with the digital camera. He cleared the screen of the other faces and put Miss Vaughn's face up there.

"And your computer is going to magically send me to Philadelphia?" Miss Vaughn said with a smirk.

"It's hooked up to the Anytime Anywhere Machine under my bed."

"Qwerty, don't," Joey warned more forcefully.

"She asked for it," Qwerty said as he pushed the ENTER key.

Miss Vaughn disappeared.

In Philadelphia, it had been a long day for Benjamin Franklin. While younger delegates were out celebrating the completion of the Declaration of Independence, Franklin walked home slowly, ate his squirrel stew, and curled up with a book in his bedchamber. That's where he was when Miss Vera Vaughn landed in the middle of the floor.

"Eeeeeeeeeeek!"

"Miss Vaughn!" Franklin exclaimed, a welcoming smile spreading across his face. "To what do I owe the pleasure of your company this evening?"

"Where am I?" she asked, dazed.

"Philadelphia, of course."

"In seventeen seventy-six?"

"July the fourth, to be precise."

"So that machine Qwerty has under his bed actually works?"

"It most certainly does!"

Miss Vaughn looked around the room for a moment, trying to comprehend what had happened to her. Satisfied that it was not all a big hoax being played on her, she turned back to Franklin, sitting naked in his chair. "What are you doing?" she asked.

"Taking an air bath," he replied.

"A *what?*"

"An air bath. I find it most invigorating to sit in my chamber without any clothes whatever, half an hour or an hour, according to the season—either reading or writing. Would you care to join me?"

"Mr. Franklin!"

18

Grounded

"Dinner!" Mrs. Stevens hollered from the bottom of the stairs. "Time to wash your hands for dinner!"

Qwerty, Barbara, and Joey came downstairs. Madison was still setting the table. Mr. and Mrs. Stevens looked at the boys and burst out laughing.

"What's with the funny clothes, guys?" Mr. Stevens asked.

Qwerty thought about making up a story to explain the colonial clothing they were wearing. But lies usually got him into trouble, so he decided to just be honest. "Uh . . . would you believe that Benjamin Franklin gave them to us?"

Barbara shot Qwerty a look.

"Hahaha!" Mr. Stevens laughed. "That's a good one!"

Mrs. Stevens invited Joey to stay for dinner, but he said he had to get home. Qwerty walked his friend to the door, half expecting Joey to punch him or something for all the trouble they had been through during the day.

"Sorry about . . . everything," he whispered.

"Are you joking?" Joey replied. "This was the coolest thing that ever happened to me!"

"Pick me up for school in the morning?" Qwerty asked, holding open the screen door.

"Yeah," Joey replied. "Hey, when are you gonna bring her back?"

"Bring who back?"

"Turkey Neck."

"Oh, her," Qwerty remembered. "I don't know. Maybe I'll bring her back on Thursday, after school. So we'll miss the history test."

Both boys laughed.

"So long, Elvis!" Joey said, jogging down the sidewalk.

The chicken casserole was already half finished when Qwerty got back to the dinner table. He sat down, and his mother told him he looked cute in his colonial clothes.

"Are you all dressed up because of that report you had to do on the American Revolution?" Mrs. Stevens asked.

"Oh, yeah," Qwerty replied. "I think Miss Vaughn might give me extra credit."

"Wonderful!" his mother exclaimed. "I never even saw you working on it."

"Well, I work fast."

"You'd better start studying for the test you have on Thursday."

"Uh, I think it might be postponed, Mom."

"So, how was your day, Barbara?" asked Mr. Stevens, who always liked to ask everyone how their day was. "You were sick this morning. Are you feeling better?"

"Oh, yeah," she said, shooting Qwerty another look.

"Today in school we learned about all the words that start with the letter *M*," Madison announced.

"Marvelous!" Mr. Stevens enthused. "That's one of them. How about you, Qwerty? Anything exciting happen today?"

Qwerty stole another glance in Barbara's direction. "Nah," he said. "It was pretty boring."

"How did your doctor appointment go?"

"Uh . . . Dad. About the doctor appointment . . . I forgot to go."

"You forgot to go?!" his father said, alarmed.

"How could you forget to go?" Mrs. Stevens asked. She shook her head. She always tried to be sensitive, but it was sometimes hard to understand how Qwerty would manage to forget so many things.

"Is Qwerty going to get in trouble?" asked Madison, who loved it when her brother or sister got in trouble.

"This is serious, Qwerty," his father said, with his *this-is-serious* face.

"I'm sorry. I—"

"I suppose you had something more *important* to do," his mother said, sarcasm in her voice.

In Qwerty's view, preventing Ashley Quadrel from turning the Declaration of Independence into a Declaration of Loyalty was a lot more important than shooting the breeze for an hour with a psychologist. But he didn't think his parents would go for that explanation. "No," he replied. "I just forgot."

"You're thirteen years old!" Mrs. Stevens said, exasperated. "You've got to be more responsible, Robert!"

"I'm sorry."

"You realize there will have to be consequences," his father said. "That's the only way you'll make the effort to remember things."

"I know."

"You're grounded for a week," Mr. Stevens said sternly. "Except for school, you are not to leave your room."

"Oh, man!" Qwerty complained.

But when his parents weren't looking, he fired a wink at Barbara and wondered if she was thinking what he was thinking.

Grounded for a week? Stuck in his room?

Ha!

This will be a good week to crank up the old Anytime Anywhere Machine.

A Note from the Author
Truths and Lies

Everything in this book is true. Except for the stuff I made up.

I learned a lot about Benjamin Franklin and the American Revolution by reading *Franklin of Philadelphia*, by Esmond Wright; *Benjamin Franklin: A Biography*, by Ronald W. Clark; *Benjamin Franklin: The New American*, by Milton Meltzer; *The First American: The Life and Times of Benjamin Franklin*, by H.W. Brands; and *American Scripture: Making the Declaration of Independence*, by Pauline Maier.

I tried to blend fact and fiction to write an

entertaining story that would also make Benjamin Franklin come to life.

Truths:

•Franklin *did* invent an electrical battery that could deliver powerful shocks, and he also invented a musical instrument called the Armonica in 1761. It was a fad for a time, and Mozart and Beethoven both wrote music for it.

•Franklin *did* have a falling out with his son when William remained loyal to England. During the Revolution, William was actually sent to prison in Connecticut and he died in poverty in 1813.

•Franklin really *did* take "air baths," though they were frowned upon by most people. Most people in those days thought fresh air was bad for you.

•Street names, locations, and facts about Philadelphia, Independence Hall, Franklin's house, and the Liberty Bell are all true. Much of Franklin's dialogue is actual quotes by him. And Franklin *was* known to be quite the ladies' man.

Lies:

•Everything about Qwerty, Joey, Ashley Quadrel, and the Anytime Anywhere Machine is fictitious.

•While July 4, 1776, is probably the most famous date in American history, there is actually very little written description about what happened in Philadelphia that day. There is even some disagreement over when the Declaration was signed.

Most historians say it was approved on July 4, signed by John Hancock that day, and sent out to be printed. Then, on August 2, the other delegates returned to Philadelphia to sign the handwritten copy. However, Thomas Jefferson wrote in his own notes that the Declaration was signed on July 4, so that's good enough for me.

By the way, the orignal Declaration of Independence is lost, and only twenty-five copies of the printed version survive. In 1989, a man found one hidden behind a painting he had purchased at a flea market for $4. He sold it for over $8 million.

Even though he was an old man in 1776, Benjamin Franklin's career was not finished. He sailed to Paris that year to enlist the help of the French in the American Revolution. When returned to Philadelphia nine years later, he helped draft the Constitution. Many believe it was

Franklin's idea to satisfy both large and small states by giving each state an equal number of senators while numbers in The House of Representatives were determined by the population of each state.

Benjamin Franklin spent the year 1789 in constant pain from kidney stones and died at age eighty-four on April 17, 1790. He is buried in Philadelphia, two blocks from Independence Hall.

John Adams and Thomas Jefferson died within hours of each other on July 4, 1826—the fiftieth anniversary of the Declaration of Independence.

Benjamin Franklin Chronology

1706: Born in Boston on January 17. He was the fifteenth of seventeen children and the youngest of ten boys.

1723: Runs away to Philadelphia.

1728: Opens his own printing company.

1730: Marries Deborah Read.

1731: Begins publishing *Poor Richard's Almanack*.

1737: Appointed postmaster of Philadelphia.

1742: Invents what becomes known as the Franklin stove.

1747: Begins experiments with electricity.

1748: Retires from business.

1749: Constructs first electrical battery.

1753: Appointed deputy postmaster general of North America.

1756: Appointed postmaster general of the colonies.

1757: Moves to London as an agent for Pennsylvania.

1762: Returns to Philadelphia after five years in London.

1765: Returns to London, works to repeal the Stamp Act.

1766: The Stamp Act repealed.

1774: Wife Deborah dies.

1775: Returns to Philadelphia. The Battle of
Lexington and Concord is fought as Franklin
sails home. Elected to the Continental
Congress.

1776: Helps draft the Declaration of Independence.
Sails for Paris, where he will live for nine
years.

1778: Negotiates treaty of alliance with France.

1779: Appointed minister to France.

1782: Negotiates peace treaty with England (with
John Adams and John Jay).

1785: Returns to Philadelphia. Invents bifocals.

1787: Helps draft the Constitution.

1790: Dies at 11 P.M. on April 17 in Philadelphia at
age eighty-four.

Just some of Benjamin Franklin's achievements

Author and publisher of the best-seller *Poor Richard's Almanack*
Printed the first political cartoon
First to use questions and answers in journalism
Founded the first circulating library in America
Organized the first hospital in America: Pennsylvania Hospital
Established the University of Pennsylvania
Founded the first American fire insurance company
Established the American Philosophical Society
Organized the first militia in Pennsylvania
First postmaster general of the United States
First to identify lightning as electricity
Invented the Franklin stove
Invented the lightning rod
Invented the first electrical battery
Invented the catheter
Invented the odometer
Invented bifocal eyeglasses
Invented the first musical instrument by an American
Proposed what came to be known as daylight saving time

First to recognize that white clothing reflects heat;
and dark clothing absorbs it

Charted the Gulf Stream

Member of the Continental Congress

Signer and coauthor of the Declaration of
Independence

Signer and coauthor of the United States
Constitution

American minister to France

President of the Pennsylvania Society for
Promoting the Abolition of Slavery

About the Author

Dan Gutman is the author of *The Kid Who Ran for President, Honus & Me, The Million Dollar Shot, Johnny Hangtime,* and many other books for young people. *Qwerty Stevens, Stuck In Time With Benjamin Franklin* is the sequel to his novel *Qwerty Stevens, Back In Time: The Edison Mystery.*

To find out more about Dan Gutman and his books, visit his Web site (www.dangutman.com).